PHANTOMS OF THE FORT

R.G. HILSON

PHANTOMS OF THE FORT

By R.G. HILSON

Phantoms of the Fort

Paperback: (979-8-950072-30-7)
Hardcover: (979-8-950072-31-4)

Table of Contents

Foreword

If you intend to visit an old British Fort in Ontario or in New York and you don't believe in phantoms, you've got to ask yourself just one question.

Do you feel lucky?

Phantoms of the Fort

Danny Hood was anxious to tell Alan about a dream he had the night before. But it didn't look like a good time to talk since their father was outside waiting for them. He had already chided them for being tardy. As usual, Alan was taking too many books on the trip with him. Danny, on the other hand, couldn't figure out what he wanted to take. He finally decided that Alan was taking enough for the two of them.

Sarah Hood came out of the house with her white purse in her arms, saying how warm it was. Sarah was about thirty years old and slim. She had beautiful long black hair which curled up in ringlets when it was wet. Today she was wearing a dazzling south sea islands type of print dress, in patterns of white and red flowers that didn't match the mood she was in. She was getting a little annoyed at her husband for spoiling the day's outing with his usual gripe about everyone being late for their own funerals.

As soon as both of his parents were out of earshot, Danny signaled Alan to join him beside their father's car. Danny didn't want to keep his father waiting any longer, but he needed to speak to someone about something that had been bothering him all morning.

"Alan, I had a strange dream last night about meeting someone at Fort Erie today," Danny said to his older brother.

"That sounds weird, Danny," Alan replied. "You've never been to that fort before and you don't know anyone who has."

"I think it was an older soldier who I was talking with," Danny insisted.

“I thought they only hired students at the fort during the summer holidays. Maybe this fellow was an older student. What am I talking about? Danny, I think your imagination is running away with you again. Since when could you foretell the future? Let’s get into the car before Dad gets here.”

Alan opened the vehicle’s back door. Danny got in first and slid over to the other side. Alan placed his backpack beside Danny and jumped in himself. Alan didn’t waste any time. He started to unpack some of the books and games that were next to him in preparation for the two-hour drive to Fort Erie on Lake Erie. After a minute or so of fumbling, both boys were immersed in their activities and waiting patiently for their parents to get in the car with them. However, their parents were now both involved with planning the garden for next year.

“Hey Dad, we’re ready,” Alan shouted safely from the back of the sedan as he winked at Danny.

“Then what are we waiting for?” his father replied, as he went over to the front door of the house and locked it. “Has everyone got everything they need?”

The entire family seemed relaxed now. The day was turning a bit hazy and overcast as the Hoods sped out of their driveway. Their destination was Old Fort Erie which was just across the lake from the U.S.A. Two hours later, Danny watched in amazement as the old grey stone fort came into view along the open shorelines of Lake Erie.

“Dad, Fort Erie doesn’t look at all like the old log forts,” he said.

“It did at one time, Danny,” his father replied, “but it was replaced by a permanent stone structure. In fact, this was the first permanent British Army fort in Ontario,” he added.

Richard Hood was pleasantly surprised to find plenty of places to park while he maneuvered his vehicle onto the crunchy stone bits that covered the wide, expansive graveled lot. The journey to the historical fort was almost complete. The only snag was the ongoing search for the perfect parking spot.

That would be the one with the best view of the old stone fort. After finally parking the car, Richard rewarded his family for their "patience," by handing out some of the cold pop that had been stored in the trunk.

After gulping their drinks down at record speed, Richard indicated that they needed to obtain their entrance tickets at the souvenir shop. The souvenir shop was located within a rather large, modern structure built close to a fort which was hundreds of years older. There was the usual reminder that there were no modern facilities within the fort and that everyone should use the washroom before the fort visit.

By the time Richard had his entrance tickets in hand, his family had become preoccupied with multiple items of interest within the modern building. He was satisfied that Sarah and the boys would continue to investigate the bookshelves for a reasonable amount of time. This minor delay presented an opportunity for him to turn his attention towards the historical items on display in an adjoining room. After a brief visit to the adjoining room, his reaction was a feeling of wanting to dig deeper. With a better sense of awareness, he might discover something more than what one might expect while touring the old fort. Still, he didn't know exactly what that something could be.

On the other hand, Sarah knew exactly what she was looking for within the souvenir shop. She found a book that contained all the necessary information she required in order to show Danny and Alan how the fort had evolved.

Richard returned to the main part of the building. He saw that the boys were interested in a book that Sarah had picked up. He decided to join them. Richard glanced at the picture of the old fort that Sarah was showing them and launched into an impromptu presentation based on his own artistic impression of the fort.

"When you look at the fort's outline from the top, the old fort looked like a flying bat. The current fort looks more like a sea turtle trying to get back into Lake Erie. I think that tells you something about how the times have changed, boys," Richard said.

The boys started to twist their heads and nod in agreement with their father's brilliant perception of the fort's floor plans. However, Sarah wasn't about to get left out of this one.

She jumped back into the fray with, "Why do you boys think they called this place Snake Hill over here beside the fort?"

Everyone just stood there speechless for a moment.

"Let me guess," Alan finally said, "some snakes crawled up the hill."

"That seems feasible to me as well," Richard joined in.

"Me too," Danny said, "I think those snakes might have helped the British protect their fort from the Americans. If I were an American, I wouldn't want to climb anything called Snake Hill to get to the fort."

"Yes Danny, it's a great tactic calling it Snake Hill," Richard said. "Those are very insightful interpretations, boys. What do you think Mother?"

Because she thought they were making fun of her, Sarah had moved on to another book. She was looking at a watercolor showing the migration of wild pigeons at Old Fort Erie in the spring of 1804. Several soldiers could be seen firing their long muskets at numerous flocks of birds. In the background, a large Union Jack flew over a low-level building that was located close to the lake's shoreline.

"Yes, I imagine there was a great deal of wildlife around back then. Wasn't their favourite pastime shooting wild pigeons?" Sarah replied.

"Sarah, I think you cheated. What kind of book are you reading now?" Richard asked.

“Oh, it’s only an art book of some sort or another,” she replied with a sly smile.

“Okay, boys, I think we’ve had enough of this bantering about,” Richard announced, realizing that Sarah could be rather persistent. “Let’s say we start to head over to the fort. Does anyone want to check out the display room first?”

Richard gave them sufficient time to investigate all of the displays. Once he was satisfied that they were ready to move, he stepped out the back door. Sarah took the hint. She ushered the boys towards the display room exit door after noticing that their father had left the building.

Sarah and the boys headed up the path towards the fort and found Richard standing alongside a “real life” Iroquois, just outside the main gate. The native warrior invited the Hoods inside the fort for the musket firings. The family followed the native warrior through the main gate and formed up with a regular British redcoat and a soldier of the local militia. The native warrior let the two boys hold his musket. The musket was handed back to the warrior re-enactor after comments about its weight. The warrior continued to explain how both the musket and the bayonet were used in battle with a final illustration given on how to load a musket. The military drill concluded with an order to discharge all firearms.

After the musket demonstrations, all the children were given an opportunity to try on the complete British Army uniform circa 1812. The headdress was the most impressive aspect of the uniform. It added over a foot in height to everyone who tried it on. The shoulder straps, the backpack and the cut of the uniform gave the impression that the soldiers had broad shoulders. Intimidation was half of the battle. Sarah took pictures of Danny and Alan with the cannons, in uniform, holding real muskets. The pictures would provide good memories of the two boys looking fit for duty.

The fort activities were practically finished, as Sarah and Richard came down the stairs from the officers’ lodgings. Most of the tourists had left, so it was an ideal opportunity to speak casually with the staff. Richard engaged a tall, athletic British soldier and Sarah spoke to a "wife of a soldier" re-enactor, who was a local high school student. Alan was with Richard, but Danny was not in sight.

"Yes sir, I couldn't handle that job anymore. Every time I went up there, the bed was unmade ten minutes after I had made it. It was very queer," the soldier said.

Richard took a picture of the soldier and Alan together and went looking for Sarah. He assumed that Danny was also with Sarah. Then he spotted Sarah coming out of a building below the officers' lodgings. Sarah seemed to be excited about something. She had just spoken to the female student about the ghost upstairs. Apparently, the student had to ask the ghost for permission to enter the upstairs bedroom each morning. After she was allowed to enter the bedroom, she would explain to the ghost that it was necessary to make the bed. Apparently, the ghost slept in the bed every night just like a normal person would.

"Fancy that, would you?" Sarah exclaimed.

"Hey, I thought Danny was with you?" Richard asked.

"I think Danny is still upstairs in that bedroom that I was just telling you about. Wait a minute. There he is now, coming down the stairs."

"Sorry Mom; I didn't mean to worry you," Danny apologized. He quickly pulled Alan aside, so his parents wouldn't hear him. "Alan, I just met the man that I dreamed about last night. His name is Captain John and when I told him goodbye, he said, see you there."

"Who is Captain John?" Alan asked.

"Captain John is the ghost who lives in that room we just saw. He says he doesn't like people making his bed up every morning, but he realizes that the war is over and that there are many people who need to come and see the fort. He likes to see the American tourists come to his room, so he can give them the cold shoulder, as he calls it."

"So how come we couldn't see him?" Alan continued.

"He didn't want to spoil things by appearing before all of us. Anyhow, I met him in my dream remember? He seems to know all about us and our interest in the fort. He says that something special is going to happen to us later this year as well."

"What could possibly happen later?" Alan inquired.

"That's the surprise," Danny replied.

"Well Danny, did you meet a ghost?" his father said with a laugh. He had been eavesdropping on Danny the whole time. "Maybe you'll meet a few more ghosts at Fort George tonight."

"I hope not Richard," Sarah said in a grave tone of voice. "They have no electricity at the fort and it gets very dark there at night. Maybe you forgot about the children staying up all night in the event of a spooky ambush."

"We have to live a little too Sarah. You still won't let me show those old Universal monster movies to the children, in case they stay up all night, remember?"

"That's what I mean. You did show one of them, remember? Alan was afraid to be by himself for years because of Big Frank," Sarah retorted.

"I thought that movie was a comedy. I didn't think Big Frank would scare Alan at all. In fact, I thought Dracula and the Wolf Man were more frightening."

"Really? It's hard to put yourself in the place of a child. They have many more fears than we do," Sarah explained.

"So how come Captain John didn't scare Danny?" Richard asked.

“Because Captain John was a person, not a monster,” Sarah insisted. “Also, we don’t know for sure if Danny saw a real ghost, since he is the only one who saw it.”

“Does that make the ghost any less scary?” Richard suggested.

“I guess it depends,” Sarah replied

“Famous last words; let me guess. It depends on how spooky your surroundings are. Boys, you won’t be frightened at Fort George tonight will you?” Richard asked.

“Of course not; we’re use to ghosts now, aren’t we Dad?” Danny said.

“Well, let’s say that some of us are not as comfortable with the unknown,” Richard replied.

With that thought in mind, Richard got everyone together and headed down the road towards Niagara-on-the-Lake, the most haunted place in Canada.

The ghost tour was set to begin at dusk. By the time the Hoods had arrived at the Fort George parking lot, the tall canopies of old trees had hastened the transformation of day into night. Richard peered through the darkening woods. He noticed a fleeting, cloaked figure with a lantern, leading a small group of people across a narrow bridge, towards the fort.

“That must be the first group,” Richard said. “They told us that there would be two groups tonight. Let’s line up for the second one.”

Over in the far corner of the gravel parking lot, they could see a different group of people gathering. There didn’t appear to be any children present, but there were at least twenty people ready to take the tour. The tour guide was tall and slim. He was wearing a hooded cape and holding a candlelit antique lantern. He added that he would wait a few more minutes for the late arrivals; then he would proceed. Richard bought his tickets from the guide. The guide thanked him and said that before the tour was to start that anyone who experiences anything unusual might want to come forward and share it with the rest of the group. However, the rule for the Fort George ghost tour was that all participants should wait until the end of the tour before speaking about any ghosts being present and accounted for. Being scared by a ghost was one thing. Being scared by a crowd of hysterical tourists in a dark fort was quite another.

The cloaked tour guide finally bolted leaving the group somewhat bewitched. As they watched him dash away from the darkening parking lot, his lantern seemed to shrink in size. After racing ahead of everyone, he stopped outside of the fort's palisade and waited patiently for everyone to mill around his glowing lantern. Once he was satisfied that everyone was assembled, he began with a brief reminder about the haunted battlefields in the surrounding area.

"The violence of the War of 1812 had attached itself to the Niagara area like a sponge. There were many bloody skirmishes and many deaths. Many of the soldiers and other citizens had considered this area to be their permanent home and for many of them, it would remain so," the guide proclaimed.

The guide also cautioned the ghost tour participants about leaving the fort after everyone was inside. There was a dangerous moat going around the fort that one could easily step into without proper lighting. The expectation was that everyone on the tour would stay together as a group, as opposed to finding oneself groping in the dark.

By now, there was a sense of excitement. For others, a sense of unease. After going over the fort bridge, it took a few minutes for the tour group to adjust to the darkness. Once they were within the confines of the fort, the gate was quietly locked behind them.

The tour guide used the counterintuitive strategy of playing both ends against the middle as a timing devise. Before entering the fort, the tour guide had tried his best not to create any unnecessary apprehension about going on the ghost tour. That's why he never mentioned anything about the fort's ghostly inhabitants. Now that the gate was locked and his group was inside the fort that was another matter altogether.

The guide quickly got everyone into a blockhouse that housed the enlisted British soldiers. All of the tour group participants scrambled for seats along a couple of long benches. Danny found a seat in front of an old bunk. As soon as he could settle, he thought he could hear whispering, but there was no one talking near him. Then he felt something touch his ear from behind. He turned around with a start and discovered it was only a towel hanging from the bedpost.

There wasn't a sound, as the guide quickly lit a few more candles throughout the darkened blockhouse. Behind the flickering candlelight there was now a sense of a previous time among the moving shadows. After captivating the entire group with the ambiance of the blockhouse, the guide turned and pointed at the stairs leading up to the second floor.

"On these very stairs, not long ago, there was a little girl listening to my tales of the fort. Her name was Elizabeth." The tour guide paused; then he continued. "However, no one noticed the girl until right near the end of the story. You see, Elizabeth is the residential ghost here. She likes to play and tease just like any other nine-year-old child."

Everyone sat spellbound after listening to the blockhouse ghost stories, until it was time to move on to the next station. Danny sat still, until everyone had left. He could still hear whispering, and he was wondering if anyone else could. He stared into the pitch-black blockhouse but could see nothing. He felt another tug on his ear. Only this time it felt like someone or something had deliberately pulled it.

"Ouch; hey, what's going on? I hope you're not a bad ghost," Danny said out loud, as he jumped up and moved towards the doorway.

In his mind he could hear whispering again, as if someone had spoken back to him. He turned around half expecting to see a ghost sneering down at him or trying to pull his other ear perhaps. Instead, he received another message. This time the voice was very clear. It was the voice of a young girl.

"I've been waiting a long time for you, Danny. My name is Elizabeth. See you there."

Danny stumbled out of the blockhouse. It was as if someone was holding him from behind, only to let him go like a rubber band. He looked like he was fighting a swarm of mosquitoes, as he twisted himself to regain his balance. He felt a little foolish as a few of the tourists looked at him like he was some kind of troublemaker out to spoil their fun for the evening. After all, it was hard to be scared when someone was making a joke of it all.

"Hey, Danny," Alan called out from just beyond the blockhouse. "I'm over here."

Danny seemed surprised that his older brother was being so casual about it. Maybe he didn't really think that Fort George was haunted. Perhaps he could prove it to him. After all, he made a few ghost friends today.

"Would you like to meet my friend Elizabeth?" Danny asked Alan.

"Come on, Danny. Quit kidding. There are no ghosts here. The tour group is moving towards the south blockhouse tunnel. If there are any ghosts in this fort, that's where they'll be hiding."

Danny thought to himself that perhaps it was a sign of old age. Alan wouldn't know a ghost if one sat on his head. He was already becoming too rational in his thinking. He wasn't going to see Elizabeth now because he wasn't expecting to see her. Perhaps a dark tunnel would do the trick.

"Alan, I don't know how we're going to see any ghosts in that dark tunnel. If the man holds up the lantern and lights everything up, then the ghosts might not appear."

"Hey, Danny, everyone knows that ghosts like dark places like old tunnels. Haven't you read any good ghost stories lately?"

"Mom has been reading me a few, but they're not very scary. She doesn't want me to stay up all night. She doesn't want a repeat of Big Frank. Do you remember that time when you were afraid to go to bed after you saw Big Frank on the television?"

"What do you mean Danny? I was only six years old when I saw that movie. I was a lot younger than you."

"I'm a year older than you were when you watched Big Frank and I'd like to see that movie too. I guess you wouldn't mind watching it again now that you're ten years old," Danny said.

"Well, I wouldn't say that."

"It's a good thing you didn't see Dracula when you were younger. That's the one that put Dad off going into the basement on his own when he was young," Danny said.

"Boys, your father and I are over here," Sarah called out. "Our group is halfway to the tunnel by now while you fellows are having a fireside chat about ghosts."

"Sorry Mom, I had to wait for Danny. I think he was checking out the ghosts back in the blockhouse," Alan said.

"You two gave me more of a scare than all of the ghosts of the fort. I was talking with your father about some spooky stories that I had read when I realized that neither of you were within sight. Your father seems more intent on seeing a ghost than all of us; so he wasn't paying attention to where you were. You children need to mind yourselves better than usual, or you are going to end up with a scary surprise. You might even get locked up in the fort tonight all by yourselves if you're not careful."

That did the trick. Both Danny and Alan took off like a shot towards the tunnel which leads to an octagonal shaped blockhouse. The southbound path they were following was hilly. It went upwards towards the fort's palisade and than it looped back to a lower area of the fort that was well protected and hidden. The powder magazine and the tunnel were both down there.

Both of the boys turned their attention towards the tunnel. It was not a good place, Danny thought to himself. Mom had a real fright there, the last time they had visited the fort. They had gone through the tunnel and outside the fort's palisade, to a spiral staircase which took them up into the most haunted blockhouse in the fort.

After visiting the look-out on the top floor, Danny's father was the first to come down the staircase to the second floor which was on ground level and one floor above the tunnel. His father thought it was strange that the gate entrance to the fort had been left open, given that it had been shut when he passed by it on the way to the top floor; so he decided to investigate.

Sarah had followed her husband through the gate, but she ran right into it. She was shaking so much that she couldn't move. Richard became very angry. He told the ghost to get out of the way. Unfortunately, Danny was right behind his mother. He was taken by surprise as his father began to shout in his general direction. Danny jumped two feet up into the air and perhaps the ghost did too. Everyone got out of there as quickly as possible.

"Hey Danny, wake up and stop your day dreaming," Alan said. "Do you want to check out the powder magazine? Perhaps there's a ghost guard on patrol tonight and we'll be the first to spot them."

"Not now Alan. Mom and Dad won't be happy. The tour group has probably gone into the tunnel without us. Maybe we should wait for Mom and Dad to catch up."

“Well, let’s just go a little bit into the tunnel. That can’t do us any harm,” Alan replied.

“Okay, let’s go,” Danny agreed.

The two boys stepped into the opening of the tunnel. From deep within they could see a small light at the far end. The golden rays of weak light from the guide’s lantern could not permeate the round walls of the large cryptic tunnel. The guide was telling his group about the occasion when ghosts were seen coming from the tunnel into the fort.

“Mom won’t go near this tunnel,” Alan whispered to Danny, as he turned to walk out. “It’s much too dark.”

The two boys stood outside of the tunnel waiting for their parents, when Danny discovered that they were not alone.

“There are soldiers down there Alan,” Danny exclaimed, as he pointed towards the powder magazine. “I thought this was a real ghost tour. I hope they’re not pretending to be ghosts.”

“What are you talking about Danny? I don’t see anyone.”

“Look down there by the powder magazine. There are several soldiers. I can see them. I’m going down to take a look.”

“Hold up Danny. Don’t leave without me,” Alan pleaded.

Danny ran down the hill from the tunnel towards the powder magazine. The full moon had come out from behind a dark cloud and the soldiers seem to be shimmering with white light. One of the four soldiers spotted him and turned towards him. He seemed a little older than the soldiers that Danny remembered from the summer before. He didn’t seem to be surprised to see Danny either.

“Hello Danny,” the soldier said.

“How do you know my name,” Danny asked.

“I know you,” the soldier replied.

Before Danny could say another word, the four soldiers walked straight into the powder magazine through thick wooden doors and disappeared. Alan came up from behind and made Danny jump.

“Why didn’t you wait and where are the soldiers you were talking about?”

“I guess I made a mistake Alan. Let’s go back to the tunnel,” Danny said.

The boys could see the outline of their parents by the light of the moon along the palisade as they scrambled up the hill towards the tunnel. Danny looked in the tunnel to see if the group was still inside. Instead, he saw four soldiers with muskets and bayonets charging towards him. Danny was horrified. He stepped backwards and fell over.

“Ouch! That hurt,” Danny exclaimed.

“Hey, how did that happen partner,” Alan said.

Danny got up and looked around. There was no sign of the soldiers. He forgot the cold feeling that had been running up and down the back of his neck for a brief moment, as he peered cautiously into the dark tunnel again. An eerie voice came from the dim.

“See you there Danny.”

* * *

Nevertheless, Danny’s confrontation with the ghosts at Fort George did not stop the Hoods from visiting their local fort, a few weeks later on.

“Richard, today is Simcoe Day at Fort York. They’ll be having all kinds of special events, like cannon firings, drill and mock battles. They even have a special event for children,” Sarah said.

“It’s not that far to drive, so we can just about manage it, if we get going,” Richard replied.

“Alan, Danny; we’re going to Fort York today,” Sarah proclaimed.

“Okay Mom. We’re ready,” Alan replied.

Danny wasn’t paying attention to the conversation. He appeared to be preoccupied with a ghost story book.

“Hey Danny, wake up. What do you say? You’ve been day dreaming ever since we got back from the ghost tour. I think Mom and Dad saw you getting thrown backwards by the Invisible Man. Are you sure you’re okay?”

“I’m fine Alan. Mom and Dad have already forgotten about that incident. In fact, I’ve been waiting to go to one of the forts for a couple of weeks now. This is going to be a very special day,” Danny said.

“Yes I know Danny. It’s Simcoe Day. Didn’t you hear what Mom said?”

“That’s not what I meant. I think I’m going to meet someone real special at the fort today.”

“That’s what you said last time Danny. I guess you’re going to meet another ghost.”

“Don’t you believe in ghosts Alan?”

“Well sure, but I don’t expect one to come right up to me and introduce himself in a public place in broad daylight.”

“The forts are different. You know history, Alan. Anyhow, it’s like a big, haunted house full of soldiers isn’t it?”

"If that's the way you see it, Danny. What story are you reading today anyhow?"

"I'll tell you later. Dad is getting edgy again," Danny observed, as he moved closer to the front door entrance.

"Yes, I can see that he is on the warpath again. That means it time to get in the car," Alan said, as he rushed into his shoes and fled out the front door.

Richard followed the boys out to the car only moments later and congratulated them both for being on time.

After a short drive to Fort York within the city of Toronto, the Hoods found the fort tucked away in the back of beyond. There was an expressway overpass not far from the parking lot. It seemed an unlikely place to put the fort.

"Anyhow, the fort was here first," Sarah said. "In fact, they tried to get rid of the fort. They wanted to put the expressway right through it."

"I'm sure that the soldiers who fought for the land would not have rested in peace, if the fort had been taken out," Richard replied.

"Yes, there may be something to that. There have been a lot of strange stories about weird things happening around here related to the fort. I think it has to do with the old buildings in this area," Sarah explained.

"Well, I don't expect any weird events today, related to old buildings," Richard said.

"Don't be so sure of yourself. Stranger things have happened at the oddest of times."

"You're very big into Shakespeare and that's not what he said."

"You mean the bit about there is more to heaven and earth."

"That will do, thanks," Richard said being satisfied that his wife knew her Shakespeare. "Shall we proceed to the fort Mother?"

“Yes, of course. We don’t want to miss any of the special events.”

The Hoods walked past a couple of soldiers in period dress circa 1812. The soldiers directed them to the main office where they could purchase their tickets. They were surprised to find out that there was to be a Halloween weekend at the fort during October. Sarah pressed Richard into buying the tickets in advance, since the October special events sold out fast.

“The Halloween weekend should be exciting for the children Richard. They’ll probably tell a lot of spooky stories the same way they did at Fort George. It’s not as dark here, so we shouldn’t lose the boys like we did the last time.”

“I think you stand corrected Sarah. The boys were trying to lose us. I think they were trying to find real ghosts. Sometimes I think they know more than what they are willing to tell,” Richard suggested.

“Alan, you know, Mom and Dad seem to be talking about a lot of things today. I think they’re talking about how we took off at Fort George,” Danny whispered to Alan.

“Don’t worry old man. Your secrets are safe with me,” Alan replied.

Before the Hoods could complete their tour of the fort, it was time for the British soldiers of Fort York to do their maneuvers. The soldiers ran up and down the field and demonstrated their offensive tactics. A large gun was also used in the attack. It blew out a lot of smoke and caused everyone’s ear drums to pound. Later on, the children had an opportunity to demonstrate their skills in soldiering. Each child was given a wooden rifle and put to the test. A few of the braver ones were allowed to hold a real musket.

At first Danny didn’t notice the girl with the long dark hair that seemed to get closer and closer to him, until finally she said, “hello.” She looked about nine years old and she was just a little bit shorter than he was. Her dress seemed old-fashioned with some frills and things.

“Hello yourself; are you working at the fort today?” Danny asked, being a bit taken back.

“If you call this work, I guess I am. My name is Elizabeth.”

She looked so sweetly at Danny that he didn’t notice that his skin had gone all clammy. He couldn’t seem to find the right words to say. Elizabeth was a real person, so there was nothing to worry about. This could not be the same Elizabeth that told him that she would see him later. Then he realized that he should tell her his name.

“My name is Danny. That’s my older brother over there. His name is Alan.”

“That’s a nice name Danny. Will you be coming to the Halloween weekend at the fort?”

“Yes, I believe my father has already booked us for the first night. That’s Friday I think.”

“Yes, it would be. I’ll be there as well.”

“Well maybe I’ll see you there,” Danny said, without recalling how similar his comment was to the ghostly ones that he had received.

“I’m sure of that Danny.”

“I’m going to have to go now and find my brother. Sometimes he wanders off without me.”

“That’s okay Danny. I’ll see you there.”

Danny started to move away from her. There was something about that voice which was similar to the voice which he heard at the blockhouse on the ghost tour. Elizabeth’s voice wasn’t just a sound. It seemed to reverberate inside of his head. Perhaps he was just imagining what he thought he heard her say. He hadn’t gone six steps, and he turned around to wave at her, but she was nowhere to be seen.

Danny was preoccupied with thoughts about the girl with the dark hair for the rest of the summer, but the beginning of the school year took the haunted images away from his mind for a while. He was now in grade two and he wanted to see his friends after the long summer. After a few weeks, it was like there had been no summer.

As it got closer to the end of October, the children began to prepare for Halloween. Danny's mother had brought home a couple of pumpkins for carving while his father worked on the Halloween decorations. Danny was looking forward to Halloween, but he was beginning to think that his father had picked the wrong day to visit the fort; since Halloween was on Saturday this year.

"Dad, why do you choose to go to the fort, the day before Halloween?" Danny asked his father.

"Friday is the full moon, and everyone knows that is the best time for ghosts and goblins."

"Dad, was it a full moon when we visited Fort George during the summer?"

"Absolutely Danny."

"Richard, I think that it is more by luck than judgement that you always choose the night of the full moon. Did you really know that Friday Oct. 30th was the full moon last August on Simcoe Day?" Sarah said, with her eyebrows raised.

"I have an uncanny way of knowing when it is the full moon my dear. My hair goes bristly at that time of the month."

"Just as I thought: a likely story. Danny, you can't always believe that your father knows best," Sarah said. She went over to the calendar on the wall to check the facts of the matter. "Yes, it is amazing. Your father has done it again. It really is the night of the full moon. Congratulations Father."

“Don’t forget we have to leave around 6:30 p.m. It gets dark early at this time of the year, even if the clocks don’t go back until this Sunday morning,” Richard reminded everyone.

“The ghost tour at Fort York sounds fine Dad. I can’t wait until Friday,” Danny replied.

Both Danny and Alan were both ready ahead of time to start for Fort York that Friday evening. The setting sun and the cool autumn air encouraged them to make haste. However, by the time they had reached the fort entrance, the shadows of the evening had already descended.

After entering the fort, the air from nearby Lake Ontario began to chill Danny’s bones in a familiar way. Close by, he could see the CN Tower all lit up. It was the tallest free-standing structure in the world when it was built over thirty years ago. On that night, it still held the record. In Danny’s imagination, he visualized that somewhere up there on the tower, there was a phantom Union Jack flying in honour of the old British fort below.

“Look over there Sarah,” Richard pointed out. “There’s a group leaving from the Junior Officers’ Quarters. Shall we join them?”

“That sounds good to me. Here boys, you had better hang onto these sweaters. You’re going to need them when the temperature drops,” Sarah reminded them.

The Hoods joined a large group of people gathered around a tall, jolly character with a lantern. The whole group followed the man with the lantern across the large parade grounds to the stone magazine. It was like going down a great big hole in the ground. Everyone went down some stairs and crammed into the small magazine, until there was no room left. It was also difficult to see. Danny could hear his parents and Alan, but he couldn’t see them.

The man with the lantern had stayed at the door, so he could direct more and more people into the small magazine which was great for storing army munitions, but not so great for entertaining people. After counting thirty people, he told the rest that they must join another tour. There were simply too many on this one. He was right on that account. There was not a crack between the people sitting on the long benches. The tour guide then began his tale about a real horror that had occurred at this very site in 1813, when British soldiers blew up their magazine with 800 barrels of gunpowder. Thinking that it wasn't enough to make the group nervous, he kept it up. He talked about the horses that were killed and how they keep galloping at night in certain areas around the fort.

"You can hear their hooves, but you can never see them. At certain times of the year, people have heard fighting, screaming and shouting. The best time of the year to witness all of this is tonight," he said.

Without any warning, he just walked away. It was pitch-black and it was almost impossible to move without running into someone. Everyone tried to stay calm, not quite believing that the guide would actually take the light away. After realizing that the guide was not coming back, the tour group began to find their own way out.

Danny came out of the black hole in very short steps, in between his mother and his father with Alan trailing behind. They walked up the short flight of stairs and noticed the group going off at a quick pace in order to keep up with the guide.

"That group was too large," Richard said.

"Particularly for the matchbox we just came out of," Sarah agreed.

"Hello."

The voice came from behind Danny. Everyone turned to see who it was.

"Oh, hello Elizabeth; Mom and Dad, this is Elizabeth. She was at the fort the last time we were here," Danny said.

“I think I can help you folks find a better tour. It starts at the Centre Blockhouse, than it goes to the North Soldiers’ Barracks and finally it ends at the Officers’ Quarters. It’s a very special tour put on especially for tonight. Are you interested?” she asked.

Before anyone could argue the toss, Elizabeth was striding across the parade ground at a brisk pace. Danny thought she was floating at first, but no one else said anything; so he thought it must be his imagination.

“Come on Dad and Mom. Let’s go with Elizabeth,” Danny said, as his eyes followed her supernatural glide.

“I wonder where her folks are,” Richard exclaimed. “She doesn’t appear to be with anyone.”

“She seems okay,” Sarah said. “I guess she is what some people call a free spirit.”

“Free spirit or not, we’re not going find out what she’s up to unless we get moving,” Richard suggested.

Danny thought that whatever spell Elizabeth had used on him, it was working on his parents as well. Alan just seemed to be going along for the ride.

“I just hope they don’t turn the lights out again,” Alan said, looking a bit paler than usual. “There may be city light all around us, but once you get inside these old buildings, it’s like being in another world.”

The Hoods arrived at the front entrance of the Center Blockhouse, but it looked like it was completely dark inside. The Hoods had doubts about proceeding.

“Perhaps she meant the East Magazine,” Richard suggested.

“Dad, I’m not going into any more of those tiny magazine houses tonight,” Alan spoke out, being a bit distressed from his first experience in the main one. “Unless you have a flashlight packed.”

“Alan, wouldn’t you say that bringing a flashlight to the fort might defeat the purpose of being here. Whoever heard of going to an old fort with a flashlight. Nobody else has got one,” Richard said.

“Yes Alan, it might take the mystique of the fort away. Your father is really an antiquarian at heart,” Sarah stated. “Perhaps he will change his mind if he ever encounters a real ghost.”

“Hello again; it’s me Elizabeth.”

The voice seemed to come out of nowhere. Danny thought that she might have been hiding at the bottom of the stairs in the shadows, but that seemed improbable.

“Oh, hi Elizabeth,” Danny said, hoping that he wouldn’t weaken now. “I thought you had disappeared for a minute.”

“Come on in Danny. They’re ready to start,” she said, ignoring his comment.

Inside there were plenty of wooden benches and lots of room to sit. Danny’s older brother and his mother sat near the front and his father sat further back near the door. Elizabeth sat beside him. Danny noted that her dress seemed old-fashioned like the woman at the front who was sewing, except that Elizabeth had a long suede coat over her dress. Elizabeth seemed very eager for the presentation to start and she didn’t have to wait long.

The woman in the pioneer quilted outfit at the front seemed to be sewing some type of garment. She had her hair pulled tight and wrapped up in a bun behind her head. She was rocking back and forth in an old wooden chair that creaked occasionally. Danny was amazed that she never missed a beat, with the story or with the sewing.

“Welcome to Fort York. As you can see, I’m knitting a quilt for a long and cold winter’s evening. The people back at the time of the War of 1812 had to be prepared for everything. Their survival depended upon it," the pioneer lady stated.

She went right into her story. Her piercing eyes looked up on occasion when merited. The audience was lulled into what seemed like a common folk tale, but it soon turned into something more macabre.

"This strange event took place at the beginning of the War of 1812. It's a legend among the natives because no white man has ever lived to tell this tale."

Danny wondered how this old woman would know about a native legend, untold by the white man, who never recorded it. Perhaps her family had native blood; or maybe she had made it up after all. Still her tactic worked. Any disbelief in the audience was short-lived.

"Before I begin, let me say that this is a true story, but you must decide for yourself individually, if what I say is true."

Elizabeth was in total rapture with the woman's story and so was everyone else, so far. The pioneer lady continued.

"In 1812 things were not that good in England, if you were poor and out of work. On the other hand, if you took the King's shilling and made a commitment to serve ten years in His Majesty's Army, things could improve. This is a story of someone who should never have taken the King's shilling."

To Danny's amazement, Elizabeth grasped his hand tight. He felt transported back in time to a more simple life when making biscuits, sweet breads and ice cream were special events. He recalled what he had heard not more than a few minutes before about how the pioneers had to make enough clothes to protect themselves against the elements. He wondered how he could have survived in such a place without television and computers.

"This is the story of Harry Green and the white wolf. Harry Green joined the British Army in the year before the War of 1812. It's unlikely that he would have joined, if he had known that there was going to be a war with the Americans. British discipline meant nothing to Harry. He was often in trouble with his superiors. If it wasn't for the War of 1812, his superiors would have let him desert. In fact, that is what they were hoping he would do."

Everyone laughed at that comment, but the tension in the room was starting to build quickly. Danny suddenly realized that Elizabeth had his hand in a vice grip. He let out a sharp whimper and looked at Elizabeth in a rather questioning matter.

"I'm sorry Danny. I must have got carried away. This is a rather frightening good story, is it not?"

Danny was a little surprised that Elizabeth had seemed to develop an accent that was different from the one that she had used before. Perhaps she came from England after all.

"That's okay Elizabeth. Are you okay now?" Danny asked.

"Yes, but I can hardly wait until the end of the story," she whispered, as the storyteller began anew.

"Well, it appears that Harry Green had heard some rumors about a great white wolf while stationed here at Fort York. According to native legend, the white wolf was the protector of native lands around the fort. Indeed, a white wolf had been spotted near the fort recently. Harry convinced three other soldiers to help him track the beast down. A light snow had fallen, as the soldiers headed north from the fort. It was late in the afternoon on a cold December day when the incident took place. Harry Green's three friends had already begged him to give it up because the sergeant major would have them punished, if they did not return to the fort within the hour. But Harry swore he saw the beast go into a thicket of trees not more than one hundred yards away. The other soldiers thought they also saw something large and white go into the thicket, so they decided to follow Harry. Harry disappeared into the thicket and there was an almighty crack from his musket. The others rushed to where smoke was still belching from the discharged musket not more than thirty yards away."

The storyteller stopped for a breather and looked up from her knitting.

"They stepped into the thicket and they saw a very large white wolf. They were too mortified to lift their weapons. The wolf just stood there looking at them for a minute. Then the beast turned around and jumped out of the thicket. They all swore that they couldn't move while the beast looked upon them. But when the beast left the thicket, the spell was broken and they were able to pursue it. They reached the spot where they saw the wolf disappear; but there was no sign of the wolf, or any tracks to be seen. Then they realized that they had not seen any sign of Harry either; so they began to shout out his name. They found him a couple of minutes later, exactly where his musket was fired. Harry was stone cold dead. He looked like he had been frozen for hours. But what really disturbed the soldiers was the condition of the musket. They all tried to pick up Harry's musket. Each soldier described a feeling of morbid dread, an intense sense of coldness and a loss of feeling in the hands, after picking up the weapon. In addition, it was most uncanny that the weapon had not been fired. All the soldiers agreed on that point. The soldiers were talking about what they should do with the body, when one of the soldiers looked up to see the large white wolf staring at them, not more than fifty yards away."

The pioneer lady waited for the reaction in the audience and continued with the story of Harry Green.

"They raced back to the fort in a panic and told the sergeant major their story. A search party was sent out immediately, but Harry's body was never found. The only thing they did find was the musket. The musket looked like it had been at the bottom of a lake for a thousand years. It also looked like the breach had exploded, even though there was no evidence of that before. They took the musket back to the fort to examine it," she said, as she paused to adjust the quilt.

"But the most frightening events were yet to happen. One of the soldiers dared to venture outside of the fort the next day. It was a native who found him frozen stiff, the following morning. The native claimed that the great white wolf had taken his spirit. Another one of the soldiers on the accursed hunting trip, died in his sleep three days later, after dreaming of a white wolf which had come to his bedside, inside the blockhouse. The last surviving member died on the Sunday before Christmas, after falling down some stairs. It was rumored that a white wolf was seen leaving the fort, just after the unfortunate event," she said, as she put the quilt down.

"Although rumors of supernatural occurrences continued, it was considered bad luck to speak of the white wolf, or mention anything about the soldiers who had died under such mysterious circumstances. Moreover, no one was surprised that Harry Green's musket was taken to the local shaman to have the curse on the fort lifted. After that, everything returned to normal and the soldiers could leave the fort again without fear of the white wolf."

The story ended and everyone clapped their hands in appreciation. The candlelight near the old woman seemed to go dim, as she appeared to fade into darkness. Danny just stared ahead, thinking about the story, until he hear the words, "see you there."

The words "see you there," appeared to be directed at Elizabeth, but he thought that it was intended for him as well.

"Danny, what did you think? Was that story scary enough?" she asked him.

"Yes, it was scary Elizabeth. I hope it doesn't give me nightmares tonight. I can see that big white wolf staring at me from my bedside right now."

"That's nothing. Wait until you see what comes next. Are you ready to go?" she asked without bothering to wait for an answer.

Danny noticed that the tour group he was with were dressed in old-fashioned clothing and seemed to know each other. Maybe people like to dress up when they visit old forts, he thought to himself. He never gave it a second thought, as the group moved from the Center Blockhouse, into the cool night air and made their way towards the Soldiers' Barracks located on the north-west side of the fort. Inside the barracks, there were benches for the tour group, the same as before. From behind the door a rather short soldier jumped out in full British military dress circa 1812. He lit his lantern and appeared to be drinking a bottle of wine. Danny didn't think he was really drinking, but he was as happy as a lark. The soldier's jovial square face could be seen in the lantern light, until he walked over to the darkened wall, on the far side of the barracks. Then he held his lantern up for everyone to see what was hanging on the wall.

All the mutterings and noises in the room ceased. All faces were pointed in the same direction. They were staring at the head of a magnificent stag.

"This is not an ordinary animal. This so-called trophy is haunted. In fact, it is no longer here at the fort because of the trouble it created. So, sit back, relax and I'll tell you the tale of the haunted stag's head."

Of course, everyone just continued to stare at the piercing eyes of the stag. It's silly, Danny thought to himself. How can a stuffed head be scary?

"It was one of the sergeants that killed the beast, during the War of 1812. He killed the animal on hallowed native burial grounds. The shaman warned him that if he took the dead beast with him, it would bring misfortune to him and anyone else who associated with him. The so-called prize trophy was taken to the fort. The head of the beast was mounted and placed in the Junior Officers' Quarters. Within a short period of time, every officer who was billeted there became sick or had an injury. Items of importance went missing and everything seemed to move around for no reason. The officers blamed their bad luck on the stag's head and finally decided to have it removed. The sergeant thought that the officers' theories were ridiculous. He didn't want to get rid of the stag's head, so he took his trophy down to the stone magazine in order to hide it. He found a special heavy-duty case to place the head in; then he buried the case in a secret compartment below the floor of the magazine," the soldier said solemnly, as he lowered the lantern.

"A month later, the Americans attacked the fort. The magazine blew up killing the sergeant and hundreds of other soldiers. After the blast, the Americans occupied the fort. In their investigations of the powder magazine explosion, the Americans found the stag's head undamaged. One of the American officers took the stag's head as a memento for his victory. He walked over to the stone well with it and was leaning against the well when the structure gave way. It seemed strange that both the head and the officer would both go down the well together. They found the officer at the bottom of the well, impaled on the stag's antlers. The body of the soldier and the stag's head were taken from the fort and that was the last that anyone expected to hear about the trophy," the soldier said, as he took one long swig on the bottle.

"According to the legend, on each anniversary of the explosion, the ghost of the stag's head will reappear in the well. There is only one other occasion when the stag's head will appear and that is at the end of October. No one knows why. Perhaps it is because the spirits are restless. Perhaps it is because the spirits won't rest until their tale is told. Now you know the tale. Now the spirits can rest."

Everyone seemed satisfied with the tale. It was almost a disappointment for Danny. It didn't seem like a real ghost story at all. The soldier took another long drink of his wine and stood as tall as he could. He raised his lantern up to the stag's head; but it was gone. Everyone gasped in amazement. Danny's jaw dropped.

"I hope everyone enjoyed my ghostly tale. Please proceed to the Officers' Quarters for the final ghostly tale of the evening," the soldier said.

Elizabeth seemed to be excited about getting to the final event of the night at the Officers' Quarters. "This will be wonderful Danny. You and your family are going to love this," she said as she got up to go.

"Just a minute Elizabeth, I want to talk to that soldier about something," Danny replied. "Sir, can I speak to you for one minute please."

Danny saw the lit lantern go back towards where the stag's head use to hang and he even thought he saw the soldier carrying it as clear as day, just before he spoke with Elizabeth. As he turned back towards the inside of the barracks the lantern's candle light went out.

"Sir, I'd like to speak to you about something," he repeated. Danny waited, but there was no reply.

"Sir?"

Now the light was gone and it was pitch dark inside the barracks.

"Elizabeth, I saw the candle go out, but he must still be in there."

"No Danny. There's no one inside the Soldiers' Barracks right now," was all that Elizabeth said.

Richard, Sarah and Alan were outside the Soldiers' Barracks waiting for Danny and Elizabeth.

"That's the second time you tried to stay behind. Did you guys find some real ghosts or something?" Alan asked Danny. "We don't want you to get locked up tonight, Danny; so watch out for those heavy doors that lock from the outside."

Danny didn't know if what Alan had said was true or not, but it did give him enough concern to pause on it. What would it be like to be locked up in the barracks overnight with no way out? Some of the buildings didn't have windows for security reasons. Now he was thinking that this building might provide security for the ghosts too. He felt a chill go down his spine. Looking at Elizabeth made him feel even colder. He liked her, but he always felt cold when he sat beside her. Why, he wondered?

Everyone filed into the Officers' Quarters. It was joined to a large kitchen. The main area was very comfortable with a large dining room table and a roaring fireplace. A British officer was presiding over the activities this time. When he said that he was known as Captain John, Danny couldn't believe his ears. He looked very hard at the Captain and felt that he had indeed seen this officer before.

"I hope you are comfortable, ladies and gentlemen. Tonight promises to be the most exciting Halloween celebration that we have ever had. But before we begin, I encourage you to come up to the dining room table and partake of some fine sweet breads and cookies made from a special old-time recipe."

The Captain waited for everyone to get their snack and then he continued.

"You're probably wondering about what kind of a ghostly tale I have for you tonight. But first, I must ask you to stay in your seats and remain calm when things do start to happen. Perhaps the rapid beating of your heart and some ice cold shivers is all there is to worry about after all."

Danny sat quietly thinking that it was a very strange way to introduce a ghost story. Perhaps he was trying to imitate Vincent Price, who always made being scared to death sound like it was no big deal. His parents wouldn't let him watch Mr. Price's scary movies; but he saw one about a haunted house when his parents weren't aware that it was on television. It was too bad that his father caught him watching it. His father told him about the time that he had jumped two feet off of his chair, in the air, with his hair going straight up because of the same film. It was a good thing that the movie had not got to the part where the old ghostly hag appeared in the dark corridor. Now that part would scare your pants off, he said. Well Danny was beginning to think that his father was right about the movie after all, since he was beginning to feel like jumping out of his seat right at that moment. Then Elizabeth took his hand again.

"It will be okay Danny. I'll stay here with you. No harm will come to anyone here tonight."

Danny was too embarrassed to say that he was scared of what was going to happen next. He just looked at Elizabeth like he had just seen a ghost. Elizabeth just smiled back like she was the cat that ate the canary. Satisfied that Danny wasn't going anywhere too soon, she turned her head towards the storyteller slowly with a rather smug look of victory on her face.

Alan was directly behind Danny, and he poked him in the back. Danny's back arched like a cat and his hair seemed to fan out in all directions.

"What's the matter big boy? Cat got your tongue," Alan said.

"Ladies and gentlemen, let us begin," Captain John said before Danny could regain his composure.

"My tale tonight has to do with the phantoms of the fort." Danny gulped. "In fact, we should be seeing them very shortly."

Everyone now seemed to think that it was part of the thrill, so no one looked concerned, except for Danny.

"The special haunting that will occur tonight is a result of an incident which happened almost two hundred years ago."

Danny was thinking that this Captain John was really setting himself up for failure. All of the ghost tours that he had been on in the past never promised a ghost. Many participants asked for one, but very few tours delivered. Perhaps he was getting excited about nothing after all, so he decided that he would relax and watch the show in comfort. At least that is what he thought he would do.

"Almost two hundred years ago there was an explosion here. The fort's power magazine that blew up during an American invasion in April of 1813 caused unbelievable pain and destruction. It killed and maimed hundreds of soldiers within a few short minutes. Many of the soldiers died so suddenly that they never knew what happened to them. Now I won't say why I think there are ghosts here at this fort, but I will say that on the night of the full moon at certain times of the year some say that the phantoms of the fort will appear. Ladies and gentlemen, I believe that time is tonight. Let's just say that I have certain psychic evidence which suggests that the powers of evil have been amassed tonight and that negative energy has temporarily transformed this fort into something so malignant that I must ask you to remain calm in your seat until the danger is past. Also, you may not have noticed that it is almost twelve o'clock. We don't normally do tours this late; however, you must agree that this is great opportunity tonight, to meet every evil phantom that has ever existed in this particular fort without any danger to you or your loved ones."

Danny thought that this guy must be nuts, until he asked that all of the lights should be turned down. He then reminded everyone to remain calm throughout the haunting. Danny was about to ask his father if he could leave when he saw the first ghost. Oddly, it was just like the ghost that his father warned him about. An old ugly hag, who must have been a witch, appeared at the outside window. At first, she glared in; then she heckled some witch's curse at the audience. There were plenty of screams and some people actually looked terrified. Captain John drew his sword and walked over to the window.

"Be gone old hag," he said.

The old hag vanished and it was pitch dark again. Then there was something else at the window looking in. The phantom was wearing a British soldier's uniform with sergeant stripes on the arms; but it had the head of a stag. Its great antlers banged and clattered against the window and it looked like the glass would break at any moment. Everyone seemed to be crawling backwards, as the banging of the antlers unnerved them. Captain John spoke to this phantom as well.

"Be gone phantom of the stag."

Again, the vision disappeared and everyone in the audience waited for another terror. There was some whispering and some tales of foreboding, but everyone managed to stay in their seat.

"It's now the witching time or the hour of the dead. The invasion of the fort has begun. Look now," Captain John said, as he pointed his sword towards the window.

Outside the Officers' Quarters, the bones of soldiers were fighting each other with rusted swords and muskets. Finally, there was a terrible red flash and the sound of thunder. In the moment that it took to take a deep breath, time was released. Darkness was replaced with a soft pale, radiant light that streamed into the Officers' Quarters from the window.

"Elizabeth?" Danny said. There was no answer. It was as quiet as a graveyard. "Where is everyone?"

"I really don't know Danny," his father said, sounding confused.

As the Hoods got up from their seats, they noticed that the door of the Officers' Quarters was left open for them to leave. It seemed like they were living a dream, as they left the fort. The gates of the fort were still open and there was mist rising from the parking lot, but there were no people in sight.

"We haven't been at the fort that long, have we Dad? It looks like everyone has left and gone home," Danny said, as he looked back at the fort, along side his father. "Fort York is really eerie when it's quiet. It's so strange when there's no traffic on the bridge."

"It looks like time has slipped us by Danny," his father replied. "Danny, those gates closed behind us. Unless, I'm crazy, no one was in the fort when we left."

As Danny and his family reached the parking lot, the drone of the expressway started again. Perhaps, Fort York is haunted after all, Danny thought to himself. He looked back at the fort one more time. He could plainly see the outline of a little girl waving from beside the gate. In his mind he could hear these words.

"I hope you enjoyed the real ghost tour with my friends. See you here next time Danny."

It was Elizabeth's voice.

For a Few Phantoms More

Danny aged eight had just arrived at Fort Henry; located in Kingston, Ontario with his mother, his father and his older brother for a few days during the summer. They proceeded to walk from the parking lot, to the entrance of Old Fort Henry. After reaching the parade grounds, they walked up a steep set of concrete stairs, so they could view the show from the stone balcony. The Hoods found a wooden bleacher to sit on, just as the Fort Henry military band came out onto the parade grounds playing "Rule Britannia."

The fort's artillery unit came out right after the marching band. Everything seemed to be going smoothly, expect for one thing. None of the big guns would fire, except for one. It blew out a lot of smoke, rags and rubbish. Moreover, it made everyone in the vicinity gag.

"Dad, the cannons don't seem to be doing that well tonight," Danny said.

"That's an understatement. Perhaps the fireworks will make up for it Danny," Richard Hood replied.

The crowd was still standing at the end of the ceremonials as they started the fireworks. The thunder-bursts were a good substitute for the misfiring cannons. The second volley of thunder- bursts seemed to be aimed directly at the audience. The experience was similar to being buzzed by a fighter jet, complete with exhaust fumes and jet engine flames. The Hoods expected everyone to run for cover, but no one moved, thinking that they were safer just standing there. Fortunately, the grand finale of fireworks took place without incident.

“That last thunderclap before the grand finale wasn’t called for,” Richard commented. “I wonder what went wrong. I would say that it was done very creatively in order to maximize terror.”

“Dad, I don’t think the staff, at Fort Henry want to deal with heart attack victims,” Alan suggested.

“Perhaps the ghost tour will be hard on the nerves as well,” Sarah added.

“Well, I doubt whether they can terrorize anyone like what we just went through,” Richard stated.

However, Mr. Richard Hood was wrong on that account.

Numerous brave souls who had withstood the thunderclaps during the Sunset Ceremonies were moving towards the new part of the fort in order to buy tickets for the ghost tour. There were two ladies with lanterns and two ghost tours selected to go around the fort that evening. The Hoods were selected for the first group with twenty other ghost seekers.

The tour guide took the first group to the Old Fort Henry archway. The usual precautions were issued, as she collected the tickets. She knew her stories and her facts like no one else, but there was a sense of disbelief in what she was saying.

A young boy shouted out whether he might see a ghost on the tour. The tour guide suggested that there were many unexplained things that happen in the fort which she would talk about later on.

“I don’t think she believes in ghosts,” Sarah whispered to Richard.

“Well, let’s hope she doesn’t meet one in a dark alley,” Richard replied.

Unbeknown to the Hoods, the tour guide was becoming a nervous wreck from the activities that she professed not to believe in. She asked everyone to stand close around her just inside the old fort as if there was safety in numbers.

"This arch here signifies the old part of the fort," she said. "We had an incident here last night. The security guard had just locked the front gate after making sure everyone was out of the fort. Construction work had started on the old fort's gate during the daytime, but he knew that no one would be working there at midnight. He heard some glass shatter but found nothing as a result of his investigation. He heard some glass break again, but this time, it was real loud. He called out for the person or persons to come out because there was no way out of the fort. There was no answer, so he called the police. The police came and found everything in order. They told the security guard that there didn't appear to be anybody in the fort other than himself. Just after they left, the smashing of glass started anew. The security guard called the police again and begged them to come back. Just after the police had arrived for the second time, there was a huge smashing of glass directly behind an officer's back. He drew his revolver and radioed for backup. Several police officers searched the entire fort and found nothing. The police report was inconclusive."

The tour guide seemed anxious to move on, away from the old archway. Maybe she was expecting glass to break at any time. The group walked across the parade ground to the officers' quarters. There were various preserved rooms behind large glass panels which looked more like glass tombs at nighttime.

The tour guide explained how one of the rooms in particular gave off a rather nasty feeling as a result of a hanging at the fort. In that room, one could observe the rocking chair going back and forth. Everyone stared at the rocking chair for a minute and when it didn't do anything, they moved on.

The tour group moved to the kitchen where pots, pans and large pieces of wood had been known to fly around. The worse thing was the hatchet that kept disappearing from the kitchen and reappearing somewhere else in the fort. The fort's management finally got rid of it.

"The wine room at the end of the hall was where another guide did his last ghost tour," the tour guide boosted. "No, he didn't die. He walked into the wine room and was locked in. He saw a moving shadow on the wall as he hid behind a wine cask. After what seemed an eternity, the door opened and he ran out of the room, never to return again," the tour guide said, taking pleasure in sharing the hazards of her job with the group.

The tour guide turned around and walked towards the far end of the room, away from the wine storage area. There was a very old, thick crossed metal doorway located there which was the entrance to the reverse-fire chamber. To reach the chamber, participants would need to navigate some steep stone stairs into a narrow tunnel which lead to an area outside of the fort's walls. The tour guide cautioned the group about potential hazards in using the tunnel. If anyone had a problem with confined spaces, they should remain above ground. The concrete blocks lining the floor and the walls were moist with water, so extra caution was required, as one should be prepared to walk upon the smoothly worn stones going down into the tunnel. There were also some low arches to watch for.

Those who braved the difficulties of the trip underground below the fort's walls, to the reverse-fire chamber were rewarded with fresh new tales of woe. There were tales about how some of the hangings at the fort had been botched and why the fort was not a great place to get your neck stretched. At least one hapless fellow had to be hung four times, until the hangman pulled his legs hard enough. That famous story encouraged prisoners to escape from the fort. After a few more stories like that it was time to move from the oppressive tunnel to the more invigorating open spaces, overlooking the water near Kingston's harbour. There were more stories of people drowning and spirits who refused to move on.

The tour group went back into the old fort again, to a room just across from David the mascot goat's resting place, for another blast of ghostly phenomena. The tour guide said that a ghost walks past this window in a tattered military uniform on occasion. Since the ghost always appears in a torn uniform, it upsets whoever sees it. Whenever any soldiers of the Fort Henry Guard run out to challenge the ghost, it disappears.

"By the way, when you leave this room, you might see red eyes on the way out. Relax, it's only David. Don't let your imagination get carried away," she warned the group as she turned around and left.

There were a few nervous chuckles, as the tour group shuffled from the dark room.

"Dad, Mom, Alan: could you wait a moment please? I want to see if I can see David's eyes," Danny pleaded, determined to find something ghostly for the evening.

Danny and his parents also looked for David the mascot goat, but they were unable to locate him. Danny looked back at the window in the room that they had just left which was not more than twenty feet away. In the window he could see piercing red eyes coming from under the hood of a cloaked figure.

"Dad look," Danny cried.

But the vision had already disappeared.

Richard spoke with the tour guide, after everyone had left the fort. He asked her about contacting the security guard who had been on duty the previous night. She agreed to help him because she was interested in the supernatural herself. She said that she had been doing the haunted walks in the old part of Kingston in addition to the fort tours. There were old burial grounds which had been built on recently; plus there had been a lot of renovations both in town and at the fort lately. She also said that even though the walks have nothing to do with psychic phenomenon, their ghost tour organization had received a significant number of reports and sightings of the unexplained during the last couple of weeks.

Richard asked her exactly what parts of town the reports were coming from. She stated that the haunted places were just over the bridge, not far from the fort. Richard made a mental note of the streets that she gave him, thanked her and suggested to his family that they have a quick look before they retire.

“It’s getting a bit late for ghost hunting, isn’t it? The boys are probably quite tired from the long trip today, aren’t you boys?” Sarah asked.

“Sarah, it’s on the way to the university. It will only take us an extra ten minutes,” Richard said in defense of his decision.

“It’s okay Mom. It’s not every day we can get Dad interested in taking us anywhere,” Danny said.

They left the fort and sped down a steep hill towards the old part of Kingston. After they had crossed the inlet river bridge, they ran into an area undergoing demolition. Danny could sense something very close to one of the new hotels.

“Dad, go down that street very slowly. I have a feeling,” Danny said.

The street was not well lit and the homes were large and Gothic looking. These homes were also doomed to their fate. They had been sentenced to the wrecking ball. Danny asked his father to stop the car. The full moon came out from its dark hiding place and everyone stared at one of the derelict homes that had been abandoned. The front window was broken and there was graffiti on the front door. There were two words that were written in bright red. The first word was “William” and the second word was “Henry” which was underneath the first word.

“I think a ghost wrote that Dad. The ghost’s name is William. Henry means Fort Henry,” Danny said. It was a creepy thought for the entire family to dwell on. Danny looked for other clues. He moved his eyes from the cryptic message and stared ahead at something more sinister. “Dad, do you see anything in the front window of that house.”

The phantom in the window had eyes like distant fires that burned with a sense of rage. It was the same hooded figure with the red eyes that looked at him from the fort. Danny gulped. The image faded.

“Did anyone see that?” he asked again.

“See what Danny?” his father asked.

“Oh, nothing Dad,” he replied. He only hoped that he could sleep tonight knowing there was something evil waiting for him at Fort Henry the next day; but he didn’t want to sound foolish like the security guard at the fort.

The next day, Richard dropped Danny, Alan and their mother off at the Fort Henry while he continued on to the university in order to research possible historical motives behind the recent ghostly incident at the fort. Danny, Alan and Sarah walked pass David the goat mascot into the newer section of the fort. Sarah and Alan both had to use the washroom at the same time, so Danny was able to stroll on his own over to the most southern wall, overlooking Kingston and the inlet. Even though it was a very warm day, his skin began to prickle and he felt uncomfortable like something wasn’t right.

“Hello Danny,” the voice from nowhere said.

Danny recognized that voice. But he wasn’t sure what to expect when he turned around. Would he be staring into thin air at a real ghost, or would she really be standing there looking at him with those soft brown eyes.

“It’s you again.”

“I’ll come to the point. You and your family are in danger if you remain at the fort,” Elizabeth said.

“Elizabeth, can you explain how you got here?” Danny asked.

“Okay, I can see that you’re stubborn like your father. By the way, don’t talk to me when there are others around. You’re going to look rather silly if you do.”

“Are you trying to tell me that you’re only in my mind,” Danny replied.

“This is no joke, Danny. I want you to listen for one minute. The others are going to return very shortly. I’m here to protect you and the others if I can, but you must remain sensitive to what is going on around you, so that you don't get caught in any traps."

"So how can you, a nine-year-old girl, protect me?" Danny asked.

"Well, if you haven't figured it out yet, I'm a spirit. I've materialized for you since I am your guardian; however, no one else will be able to see me."

"I figured you were a ghost when everyone disappeared at Fort York last Halloween. It was you at Fort George too, wasn't it?"

"It's about time you caught on."

"Okay, I get it. But I think my Mom is coming now."

"I'll be close by today Danny, but I'm going to be staying out of sight, so that you don't start talking to yourself," Elizabeth said as she disappeared.

"Hello Danny. Have you been all lonesome by yourself," Alan said.

"Just about," Danny said as his mother arrived.

"Do you boys want to get a uniform and a wooden rifle over by the sentry-box? I think the children's drill is ready to start," Sarah said.

During the drill, Danny spotted a shadow at the end of the long column of children. He thought it was strange that Elizabeth might line up for military drill, until he remembered her warning. That's when he realized that the shadow wasn't Elizabeth.

"You boys look sharp in your uniforms today," Sarah said, as the drill for the children finished up. "Before you put down your rifles, let's get a few more pictures with David and the sentry," Sarah suggested.

After the pictures were taken, the boys and their mother were ready to begin a full tour of Fort Henry. They joined one of the large groups going through, but decided to stop at the old school where the school mistress was teaching a lesson on Great Britain. The lesson changed to geometry as the two boys had a seat. One of the girls in the class wasn't paying attention and she had to go up to the board and draw three figures. Then she had to place her nose flush on the middle drawing, with her hands placed on the other two drawings. That got a laugh.

"Class dismissed," the school mistress said.

The school mistress was very young; but a large Union Jack at the front of the classroom gave her position the authority and respect it deserved. She noted that Danny and Alan had arrived too late for her previous class, so she asked them if they would like to stay and try their hand with quill writing. They were given ink jars and some paper to write letters. Then the school mistress sealed each letter with red wax. Danny stopped writing for a moment in order to talk with his mother; but when he looked back at his writing, he saw the word "BEWARE."

He quickly folded the paper with the writing on it and gave it to the school mistress for sealing. Sarah was still talking with the young school mistress, who was a local high school student, as the two boys decided to explore the room at the end of the hall.

"Hey Danny, this is the room that the tour guide was locked up in," Alan said, as he went into the wine room.

Danny followed right behind him. The boys were examining the old-fashioned wine barrels, when they both felt the room go cold. But before they could leave, the door slammed shut.

"Hey, someone must be playing a joke on us," Alan suggested. "Don't move Alan. Look at the shadow on the wall."

Danny pointed to a shadowy hooded figure that was walking from the door towards them, on the wall. It came closer and closer. Then the door flew wide open. Both boys ran for the open door and away from the phantom.

"Did you see that?" Alan said.

"Yes Alan," Danny said. "And I don't think Dad should hang around this part of the fort either. There could be trouble."

"Dad will be here, regardless. He's as stubborn as you are Danny and you should know that by now. The thing that bugs me the most is that nobody is going to believe us."

"There is more to this haunting; then what we know. I didn't tell you this Alan, but I saw that hooded shadow last night, here at the fort. I even saw it in town, when we went by that house last night," Danny said.

"I hope you didn't see anything else.'

"So, what if I did?" Danny challenged him.

"Like another ghost for example?" Alan said.

"Do you remember Elizabeth from Fort York?"

"Yes, I see what you mean. Is she here too?" Alan replied.

"I wouldn't be surprised if she didn't open the door for us," Danny exclaimed.

With that comment, a severe chill came upon both of the boys.

There were no further supernatural activities that afternoon, until the artillery drill. One of the soldiers ignited the fuse of a big gun which caused an explosion. There was loud boom, accompanied by a massive cloud of grey smoke. As the smoke cleared, rags and paper could be seen fluttering down on everyone's head. Danny was suspicious. He figured the soldiers would not load a big gun with all of that garbage. However, like everything else at the fort, you just carry on as you were before.

The flag lowering ceremony was the signal that the end of the day was near. Sarah and the two boys visited the gift shop on the way out. Richard would be picking them up shortly. Danny got an urge to leave the gift shop. He told his mother that he was going to the washroom. Elizabeth was waiting for him outside of the shop.

"Danny, listen to me carefully," Elizabeth said. "I want you to go on the ghost tour tonight. Your father must not plan on missing the ghost tour either. If he comes on his own after the tour is over, there will be great danger for him. There is going to be one opportunity to prevent something awful from happening later tonight and you are going to have to take some risks. You must be prepared."

"How do you know all of this Elizabeth?"

"We have certain powers Danny. You are up against something which has been building up over a long period of time. Someone is going to get hurt tonight if we wait any longer. The powers of evil are already too strong. I don't want you, or anyone in your family to get hurt; so you must do as I say.

"Does that mean that there will be ghosts during the ghost tour tonight?"

"What do you think?" Elizabeth's voice reverberated like a cannon blast in his head. Danny also felt an incredible chill come over him. "Just be prepared."

"Hello Danny. There you are." It was his mother. Danny looked beside him. Elizabeth was nowhere in sight.

"Mom we have to go on the ghost tour tonight again. I have a feeling that it's going to be real exciting," Danny implored. "Dad wants to come here later anyway. He might find out what he wants to know on the ghost tour instead."

"That shouldn't be a problem. Your father is like you. He is more interested in the ghosts of the fort than he is in the fort itself," his mother replied.

"I think the fort and the ghosts go together," Danny suggested. "Dad thinks a lot of the fort too."

They walked to the parking lot where Richard came out to greet them. Danny was almost too excited to ask his father whether he would go on the tour tonight.

"I hope you guys are ready for another ghost tour tonight. I have a plan," Richard said.

"Don't tell me you plan to exorcize the fort," Sarah said. "That would be a big job, according to last night's tour guide. I have a feeling that we're going to get the same guide again. She was about ready to jump out of her skin last night at the beginning of the tour. How on earth, can someone like that be a ghost tour guide?"

"Perhaps it's an occupational hazard. All ghost tour guides become frightened of their shadows after too many tours. It sounds like there's a high turnover here, or should I say turn around," Richard said.

"And run for it? Well, I hope she doesn't run out on us and leave us stranded in this dark fort tonight," Sarah replied.

"There's always the security guard to protect us," Richard reminded her, as Sarah moaned.

"From ghosts?" Sarah replied. "There have been a lot of deaths at the fort in the past and there are plenty of things that have happened around the fort recently. Do you still want to tempt fate? I'm sure the security guard would sooner work someplace else at night."

"We only have a few more days in Kingston. It appears that whatever is happening here is going to come to a crunch very soon. We could make psychic history," Richard suggested.

"You mean we could be history," Sarah corrected him. "That tour guide makes me so nervous that you shouldn't be surprised if I am the first one to run out of the fort tonight."

“Run if you may; but tonight, we will attend. Isn’t that right boys?”

“That’s right Dad. We’ve with you all the way,” Danny said.

“Don’t worry Mom. I’ll run with you if need be,” Alan said in sympathy.

The ghost tour hostess was looking braver this evening as she chose the Hoods to be part of her group once again.

“Hi. Didn’t you folks come on my tour last night?” she asked.

“Even though you gave us our money’s worth, it was a little shorter than the regular ghost tour because of the Sunset Ceremony. I thought it would be nice to do the regular one as well, since we are from out of town,” Richard explained.

“Well, thank you for your support. I don’t recall having anyone join me on two tours in a row. I hope tonight is an eventful one,” she said.

But she also choked on it, when she realized she was leading a ghost tour and not a interpretative bird walk in the woods. Richard suggested that maybe the ghosts would be well-behaved like they were last night. That seemed to settle her down.

Danny thought to himself that he couldn’t rely on the tour guide, if anything were to happen tonight. He would have to rely on Elizabeth instead. However, any rational person would not rely on a ghost for protection.

The tour guide took the group around the front of the fort and told some tales about Kingston’s haunted burial grounds. Then she took the group to the back of the fort near the open water and told the tale of the local folks who had drowned nearby. It was all quite scenic and cheerful. The tough part was going to be the actual fort.

The tour guide looked grim as she entered the old part of the fort. Sure enough, someone asked the usual question about whether they might expect to see a ghost. The sound of something falling onto the parade ground like broken glass made her turn pale. She suggested that there might be more ghosts inside the building. *What a strange comment,* Danny thought to himself. *She didn't even capitalize on the story of the breaking glass at the opportune moment.*

Even though the tour group moved rapidly through the officers' quarters, it struck Danny that one of the rooms had changed. All of the furniture in this particular room had been rearranged except the rocking chair in front of the fireplace. Danny stared at it until everyone had begun to move along the corridor. Danny stood there all alone for a minute, until he noticed that the rocking chair was moving on its own.

He ran after Alan to come and look at the rocking chair. The two of them looked into the glass partitioned room filled with the artifacts of the nineteenth century. This time, the room was back the way it was. Danny couldn't figure out how library bookshelves could move from wall to wall in seconds; yet, that is exactly what happened. Danny also remembered that Elizabeth had warned him that he should stay alert at all times. Perhaps he should have thought of that a moment sooner.

Danny was about to turn around and walk away, when something caught his eye. Coming down the shady part of the corridor towards him was a dark cloaked figure with crimson red eyes under its hood. Its bony thin fingers were reaching out towards him.

"Run Alan. It's after us," Danny blurted out, as he backed up, reached for Alan's arm and ran for his life.

The boys ran up to their parents, who were standing with the rest of the tour group in the kitchen.

"Behind us," Danny said, as he tried to catch his breath.

But there was nothing there. Richard cautioned Danny to settle down or they would have to leave the tour. Danny promised to behave. Alan was about to protest, but Danny shook his head at him and waved his hand to indicate that he shouldn't let on about anything that had happened. Richard joined the tour group, as they made their way towards the tunnel and the reverse-fire chamber. The boys and Sarah lingered on in the kitchen for a moment.

"Imagine that hatchet showing up in different parts of the fort," Sarah said to the boys, as she left the kitchen and went to the adjoining room.

The boys mulled that one over.

"It's okay Alan. They said that the hatchet was taken from the fort because it kept showing up in different places. How would you like to be scalped by the kitchen hatchet in another part of the fort," Danny said.

"What are you talking about wise guy? The hatchet is still here. Look for yourself. It's right over there," Alan said, as he pointed towards a hatchet embedded in the doorway.

"Who's the wise guy now Alan? There is no hatchet. Come on we've had enough scary stuff tonight," Danny replied, as he thought that Alan was just trying to spook him.

What happened next was complete chaos. All of the pots and pan flew off of the shelves along the wall. Logs of wood from the fireplace were thrown at the boys. Finally, the hatchet reappeared in mid-air and flew at the door. It buried itself dead center. The boys now had to walk pass the hatchet to get outside of the room. They were both too terrified to ask for help. They just wanted to escape. They inched up towards the door with their eyes glued to the hatchet.

They were almost out of the room when the same thin bony hand came out of nowhere and reached for the hatchet.

"Shut the door Alan," Danny shouted.

Both of the boys swung around to the other side of the door and gave the door a great heave ho. The door slammed shut and gave Sarah a bit of a start as she turned around to see what had happened.

"Why boys, don't you think that was a little hard?" she said, standing near the top of the tunnel, as she turned back to watch for the first tourist to reappear.

"Mom, if you knew what I knew, you would have left the fort a long time ago," Danny said.

"Well, we'll just have to wait for your father I'm afraid. They're coming out of the tunnel now," she said, as she spotted Richard near the front of the group.

"A most extraordinary thing happened down there Sarah. We found cooking pans and pots down in the reverse-fire chamber. Someone must have been playing a joke," Richard suggested.

The tour guide sped past them and marched across the open parade ground towards the room that was opposite David, the fort's mascot. Everyone followed in quick time towards David's quarters. Most of the provided benches in the small room, filled up quickly. Feeling quite confident with herself, the tour guide turned off all of the lights. There was an immediate sense of unease due to the cramped quarters. Danny thought that it would be easy to start a panic under these circumstances, and he hoped that no one would say anything or move.

Danny knew the routine, but he wasn't happy with the lights being turned out tonight. The tour guide increased his tension levels further, by suggesting that it would be easier to see the ragged soldier who haunts the fort with the lights out. She kept it up with a warning that David had red eyes and that they shouldn't worry if they see him when they leave. She wasn't going to let anyone out of the fort tonight without a good scare.

The story about the ragged soldier was over and the group got up to leave. Most of the tour group was across the parade ground before the Hood family had even left the room. Sarah and Alan left the room first. Richard lingered on with Danny.

"Over there," Richard said, as he pointed towards David's living quarters. "I can see old red eyed Dave glowing in the dark."

However, Richard failed to notice that the large plate of glass in front of David's living quarters also contained a moving shadow.

"Dad, I'm afraid that it's not David," Danny whimpered, as his legs refused to go a step further.

"What is it Danny?" Richard finally said.

It's a ghost. Maybe we had better run for it Dad," Danny said.

"Maybe we had better. I'm getting nightmares just looking at it. What does it want anyhow?" Richard asked himself.

At that point there was a tremendous crashing of glass in the parade ground as the image in the window disappeared. The entire ghost tour group just stood there for a minute at the old fort gate and then decided to beat a hasty retreat *en masse.* The tour guide looked back and noted that there were people still in the fort, so she came over to hurry the Hoods out of the fort. That was a mistake.

"We saw the red eyes in the window where David lives," Danny said.

"That's very nice, but the tour is over folks. I'm going to have to ask you to leave the fort. It sounds like there may be more difficulties here tonight."

As the tour guide spoke, there was another horrendous dropping of glass which seemed to come from every part of the parade ground. This just wasn't her night. Coming directly towards them from the gate of the old fort was a cloaked figure complete with glowing red eyes under its hood and bony thin hands.

She should have screamed, since it was her worse nightmare. Instead, she fainted and her glass lantern fell to the parade ground, smashing real glass this time and killing a very precious light at the crucial moment.

Elizabeth appeared as a semi-transparent spirit in front of Danny and his father while Sarah and Alan stepped back into the darkness towards the room which they had just left. Elizabeth's spirit spoke through Danny's mind and Danny communicated the message to his father.

"Dad, the spirit that has been haunting this fort is only a boy. But he is a very angry boy. His mother was married to a soldier, but the soldier died. The British Army gave her a choice. She had to marry another soldier or leave the fort. She decided to leave with her young boy. Shortly after that a terrible disease swept the local community. Everyone at the fort was spared, but both the mother and child died. The boy wanted to be a soldier like his father, but he never got the chance. So he came back to the fort in spirit form. The reason he is angry is because of the work on the fort. He believes the fort is being destroyed. The boy's name is William."

"Thanks Danny. That's all I needed to know," Richard said, as he turned to speak with the spirit of William. "William I know why your spirit haunts Old Fort Henry. The old fort is being strengthened to withstand the enemy. It is not being destroyed. Allow the work to continue and the fort will stand for all eternity."

Then the most amazing thing happened. The figure was no longer a hideous cloaked thing, but a smart-looking boy soldier wearing the British Army redcoat. The boy saluted smartly and fired his musket with a crack. Danny saluted back, just as smartly. Elizabeth was smiling like an angel, as she and the boy dissolved together in the gloom.

"Thanks Elizabeth. I'll never forget you," Danny said.

A voice from the darkness said softly, "I'm sure you won't Danny. You'll be seeing me again sooner than you think." He felt the familiar icy squeezing of his hand and she was gone.

"The tour guide," Sarah said, as she looked down on the limp body, sprawled on the parade ground. "Is she hurt?"

"Only her pride is hurt Mother. Only her pride," Richard said, as he sprinkled a bit of his water on her face from his plastic drinking container. The startled tour guide sat up, as soft pale moonlight broke through an angry dark cloud and illuminated a path for them out of the old military fort.

The Fort, the Foul and the Phantom

This ghostly adventure happened on an overnight visit to Toronto. Danny had just turned thirteen and he asked his father if he could stay overnight at an old friend's place which was located near Fort York.

Danny's father had just dropped him off at Ben's place. Ben lost no time in suggesting to Danny that they go visit the fort that very night. Danny was suspicious; but he went along with it. Why would Ben want to visit a deserted military fort at night?

It wouldn't be long before Danny found out what was in store for him. It only took about twenty minutes for them to walk to the fort.

"Over here soldier," Ben said, as he directed Danny towards a part of the wall where they could approach the fort without being seen. "Phil should be here any minute."

They entered the fort, walked over and sat down beside the Junior Officers' Barracks. Unbeknown to both of the boys, several shadowy figures were entering the fort, not far from them. Danny was just about to ask Ben about Phil, when he heard several voices nearby. It was a group of boys. Some whispered and some uttered curses.

"Yo, Ben: Is that you?" Phil asked, as he approached Ben and Danny.

"Here," Ben replied, as he stood up to face Phil.

Behind Phil there were nine other youths ranging in age from about eleven to thirteen.

“Phil, I’m curious about something,” Danny said. “I didn’t think Ben’s friends were interested in ghosts.”

“Yo, little brother; we’re not ghost busters.” Everyone started to chuckle behind Phil’s back. “Hold it down; I’m talking,” he said, as he turned around to see if his gang would quiet down. “My gang here is in the tobacco business. This is where we distribute the proceeds. Ben have you got the cash that you owe?” Phil asked Ben, as he turned quickly to business.

Phil must be distributing bootleg tobacco for someone who is a lot older, Danny thought to himself.

“Hey, you did okay Ben. Ninety dollars even. Here take another three cases and I’ll move you up to six next week,” Phil said, as he reached into his navy duffel bag for three cigarette cartons. “It will be the same deal. You will owe me ninety dollars on three cases, by next Friday. You make ten dollars on each case, same as before. Okay? It’s too dark here; let’s move over to the stone building.”

“Do you mean the Central Magazine Phil?” Danny said.

“If you say so,” Phil replied. “Hey, how do you know so much about the fort?”

“I come here with my parents every year. You may not have to worry too much about the light tonight, it looks like the full moon is coming out,” Danny said, as the full moon came out to flood the fort in pale white light. The gang followed Phil. They moved towards the stone magazine which was near the fort’s well.

“Okay, let’s shell out the rest of the goods,” Phil said, as he sat down and reached back into his navy-blue duffel bag.

Phil had dozens of cartons of cigarettes which he distributed. He was also collecting a lot of cash from his gang. Many of them began to smoke their cigarettes, once the proceeds were taken in. Danny was looking uncomfortable as the situation became more awkward for him. He tried to break the ice one last time.

"Ben told me that you saw a ghost by the well on a night like this," Danny said to Phil.

Phil just about split himself and so did everyone else. Danny thought that the gang had gone too far. Now he knew they were idiots. He was going to wait for Phil's answer and then leave. It was as simple as that.

"Hey do you guys believe in ghosts?" Phil said. "Maybe we should look down the well, just to make sure. Are there any volunteers to look down the well for some ghosts? I don't see any here, so they must be down the well."

Phil went over to look at the fort's well. His gang began to hoot and howl. A few gang members encouraged him to look down the well. He kept looking back at everyone, telling them to shut up because they were making too much noise. He went over to the well and looked down into the long dark hole.

"Are there any ghosts down there? H-e-l-l-o. If you're a ghost, come on out, whoever you are," he said.

Everyone started laughing louder than ever. Phil was also caught up in it by now and was too far gone to control his gang. He began to produce an idiot like chuckle along with the rest of them. Then everything just froze. The sound of laughter died like the air had been vacuumed. Coming out of the well was transparent; but visible, stag headed soldier wearing a blue American uniform from the War of 1812. The red eyes of the stag's head blazed at the gang like laser rays.

"Don't look at it Ben, follow me," Danny said, as he and Ben ran behind the far side of the stone magazine.

From behind the stone magazine, the two boys could hear the sounds of growling.

"Maybe there are guard dogs in the fort after all. They must have heard us," Ben said.

"That's not the sound of dogs," Danny replied. "It sounds more like wolves."

Danny peered out from behind the stone magazine. The appearance of each gang member could be described as half human and half animal. Their features appeared to be similar to the Neanderthal man, who died out centuries before. However, the members of Phil's gang didn't act like anything remotely human. Instead, each one of them had the instinctual perception of a savage animal.

The survival of the fittest mentality seemed to have taken over the group. The gang members were fighting over the cigarettes and filling their pockets with them like they were a precious commodity. The horrific sound of wailing, baying and fighting made Ben's blood drain from his face.

"They've been taken over by the spirits of the Ice Age," Danny said, after the thought came into his mind. "The police are going to be here any minute now and we're going to be arrested. You know that, don't you Ben? So I hope you're satisfied; or do you even care?"

"I hope they get here soon. I can't stand the wailing," Ben cried.

The voice came into Danny's mind again to go to the Blue Barracks which was another name for the Junior Officers' Barracks.

"Come on, we have to go. We've got one chance to escape," Danny said, as he ran towards the Blue Barracks. "Come on Ben, snap out of it. They're going to follow us, if we're spotted."

The howling gang had already re-distributed the cigarettes before the boys had time to make their play. Without anything to distract them, the two boys would be fair game running across the parade ground under the gleam of the full moon.

“They’re after us Danny,” Ben cried out. “We haven’t got a chance.”

“Oh shut up,” Danny said, as he reached the door of the Blue Barracks which was left wide open.

As soon as both boys were inside the barracks, the door shut on its own, in the faces of the Neanderthal pack and bolted itself from the inside. Now that they were safe, the boys began to investigate their surroundings. It would have been dark in the barracks, except for an unworldly soft light coming from one of the rooms.

“I’m not going in there,” Ben stated.

“You have no choice. You must enter the forbidden room. Our guardians will protect us, if we are pure in heart. Besides, the police will be here soon. You will be arrested if you stay where you are. Either you go into that room or you leave the barracks and join the Ice Age. It’s your choice.”

“That no choice. Do you expect me to join those beasts? Are you crazy?” Ben replied.

“Either you do as I say or I’m kicking you out. Is that clear? You are not going to mess it up for me,” Danny said and he meant it.

The two boys entered the forbidden room. The ghostly stag’s head hanging on the wall seemed to have a glow of its own. The boys moved slowly towards it, hypnotized by its huge black eyes shining with white light. Then the door slammed shut, moved by an invisible force and it remained that way for what seemed an eternity.

Upon their arrival at Fort York, some of the police officers thought they saw a man in a blue uniform near the fort’s well, but this report could not be substantiated. Outside of the Blue Barracks, the police found ten youths with large amounts of tobacco and cash on them, looking into the Blue Barracks and babbling on about ghosts. They were arrested and taken into temporary custody.

One curious police officer went up to the Blue Barracks' window where the youths were arrested and pointed his flashlight inside. For an instant, he thought he saw an eerie green orb coming towards him. He rubbed his eyes and looked again. It was gone. There was no mention of that particular incident in his report. The police continued to check all of the buildings at the fort for forced entry, but found everything to be secure. They left Fort York shortly afterwards.

Danny was starting to doze as he heard something like the thrashing of branches rubbing against the door. The door opened quietly without a sound. The pale moon had illuminated the spacious officers' living room in their absence. The relics of the junior officers were now visible along the timber walls, bleached in moonlight like phantom totems. Danny thought he detected a green mist turning golden near the window of the barracks, but it seemed to vanish. He was so relieved that the police had left that he had almost forgotten that Ben was standing there with the haunted stag's head on his shoulders. He pranced and he danced. He bayed and he bellowed.

"Oh shut up," was all Danny could think of.

There was a flicker in the room, then a flash and Ben was on the floor, a normal boy, sobbing like he lost his best friend.

"Ben, listen to me. I'm leaving first thing in the morning. If it wasn't for Elizabeth, we would be in jail right now," Danny said.

Ben stopped sobbing.

"I guess she's just another one of your ghost friends," Ben said, as he stood up.

"Let's just say that she's my best friend."

“Let’s just say that I think you’re nuts, ghost boy. But it’s real cold in here since we came out of that room; so maybe you can get your friend to let us out of here.”

Danny felt his hand being squeezed real hard; but this time it was a very warm hand. The door opened with some help from unseen hands and the room temperature returned to normal. Danny stepped out first; then Ben went for the door; but he received a good swift kick in the rear end from an unknown source, as he left. He also had a very chilly feeling every time he thought of Fort York or Danny Hood.

A Fort Full of Phantoms

Fort George at Niagara-on-the-Lake in Ontario had seen many years of neglect, up until the 21st century. Tourists finally came to the fort because of a growing interest in both the old British fort system and the ghosts of the past. It seemed that Elizabeth was back in demand. People came from everywhere in hopes that they might catch a glimpse of her. But Elizabeth's intention was not to make things that easy for them. She produced shadows, orbs and noises which would disturb the nervous types. But she never appeared, if anyone from the media was around. This story is about one of the rare events in which she did materialize in front of those who made fun of the fort ghosts.

Elizabeth's ghostly appearance at the fort happened just after Halloween. A group of naughty schoolboys had arrived at the fort and were expected to stay overnight. It was the first time that the fort authorities had allowed such an event. There was a generous donation given and the authorities were reluctant to turn the "gift" down. The gift was given by a well-meaning and respected gentleman, who had a son who was a bully boy. The boy bothered his father so much about sleeping at the fort with his friends that the father finally gave in. The arrangement called for the members of a special "purpose" group to stay the night at Fort George with Fort Staff, who had reluctantly volunteered to supervise both Bully Boy and his friends.

The Halloween ghost tour had gone through on Thursday October 31st and it was less spooky than usual. The brave boys, who had arrived for the sleepover, were now boasting about how they weren't afraid of ghosts, now that Halloween was over. There were even the few braggarts who planned on building up their reputations, by pretending that their stay at the fort was a terror. As things turned out, Bully Boy and his friends didn't have to pretend.

There were two problems with the evening, even before things got started. First of all, the organizers chose All Souls' Day, Saturday November 2nd on the night of the full moon, for the sleepover event.

The second problem was the weather. Even if the boys were not to meet one evil spirit in the fort that night, the weather was worse than could be imagined. The bitter north-west winds' first blast of winter added an interesting touch to the spine-chilling event. The blustery howls of dreary souls soon filled the night, until the whole fort vibrated with their inclement tunes of misfortune. Meanwhile, invisible hands tore at the roofs of the buildings and banged on the windows. Above the mayhem, the full moon laughed at the idea that mere schoolboys should undertake such a foolhardy mission on such a vile night, when they could have been in their nice warm beds at home having a nice cup of cocoa.

Any hapless individuals making the dark journey to the facilities, located outside of the fort, would have to be escorted by a reluctant staff member. There were always a few who might risk the pounding blows of a sinister wind or the torment of a deserted fort; but with no electricity, even the brave were against leaving their beds for the washroom. So, for the faint-hearted, hiding under the covers appeared to be the only sensible option.

There were a dozen boys getting ready for bed, while two Fort Staff kept an eye on things. Finally, the staff turned in and blew out the lanterns. After the lanterns were blown out, there was still a little bit of idle boasting.

Finally, midnight arrived. Everything went quiet for a minute, like the fort had cowered in expectation of some unnamed horror. At that point, all of the boys were grateful to be in bed, tucked into their sleeping bags. The restless staff soon settled down and did the same. Almost on cue, the fort recoiled, as the wail of the wind seemed to creep up the stairs and shake each boy by the ears with its icy breath. No one wanted to face the fort on their own, after the midnight hour, except for Bully Boy that is.

Bully Boy's enthusiasm was not to be dampened by the foul weather. It would take more than a windstorm to frighten him into submission under the covers. Warm cocoa was for sissies. Not only would he stand up against the phantoms of the fort, he would become the phantom. No one should be disappointed tonight. He would see to it. Then he would rally them all and drive out the evil spirits.

Bully Boy had a great idea. Even though he was starting to weaken, he wasn't going to let it pass. It was a once in a lifetime opportunity to scare the pants off of his friends. Bully Boy got out of his bunk very carefully and grabbed his duffel bag. He reached for his flashlight and walked out of the dorm quietly, to the top of the second floor staircase. He turned his flashlight on and went down the stairs to the bottom floor. The bottom floor had four large wooden tables and numerous solid wooden bunks. There were two separate staircases at both ends of the blockhouse, leading back up to the second story. Bully Boy's plan was to dress up like a War of 1812 British soldier, go up one set of stairs, scare someone and go down the other set of stairs, as fast as he could. At least that is what he thought he might do.

Bully Boy reached into the duffel bag to get his uniform. There was a tug on the back of his shirt. He turned quickly with his flashlight. There was no one there.

The first incident almost unnerved him; but before he could put on his soldier's uniform, there was another tug at his back. Again, he turned towards his tormentor and there was no such person to be found. This time he felt very cold. The blockhouse was like a freezer box.

By now, he had quite enough and had decided to give up on his foolhardy escapade. He was determined to run up the stairs as fast as possible; but something was trying to stop him. Something was holding his shirt again. This time it wouldn't let go.

Then, he saw it coming towards him. It was a large white orb which shimmered all over. The orb started to gain features. It had a head with long white strands flowing out from it. However, there were no arms or legs: just a body and a head floating a few feet from him.

Bully Boy didn't even notice that no one was holding onto him by now; since he was far too scared. He felt the scream that he wanted to utter. His mouth opened and the hair on the back of his neck stood on end. His head swung from left to right to left in disbelief.

"Noooooooo!"

But it wasn't his voice at all. It came from the second floor. There was a fumbling and dropping of feet. Everyone seemed to scramble and jump at the same time. There were flashlights darting around, until someone finally appeared. It was one of the staff who was looking for him. They found Bully Boy at the bottom of the stairs, staring into the dark.

The Fort Staff tried to figure out how Bully Boy did it; but it didn't make sense. How did he get out of his costume so fast? In fact, his soldier's uniform appeared to be put away neatly in his duffel bag; so they decided to question the other boys first.

The witnesses didn't help to explain any of the events either. One of the boys claimed he saw a soldier go down the stairs, after he woke up from a nightmare. Another boy claimed he saw a soldier go down the opposite staircase, after he was awoken by the first boy's scream.

After becoming exasperated with the conflicting stories, the Fort Staff finally asked Bully Boy about why he did it. He just said, "Ghosts. The ghosts did it."

Of course no one believed him. Bully Boy was shunned by his friends for a long time, since he refused to discuss the ghostly incident which often disturbed his dreams. Bully Boy never got use to the idea of ghosts either. Whenever he felt like pulling a prank, a windy branch would alert him to another possible ghostly appearance. Then his face would go pale and his knees would wobble. Perhaps that is why Bully Boy never entered an old British fort again or played another prank.

Bully Boy's father thought that the overnight visit at the fort had done his son a lot of good, since he had become very quiet and humble, after his eventful experience. The Fort George staff were also humbled, but less impressed with Elizabeth's shenanigans. Thanks to her and a few of her friends, no one slept a wink that fateful night.

The boys were collected first thing in the morning, and no one spoke of the phantoms again. Even the ghost tour omitted Bully Boy's story of Elizabeth's ghost, since he was in an unauthorized section of the fort when the alleged incident took place.

Elizabeth was so satisfied with her performance that she thought she might appear regularly on the ghost tour after all. But that is another story.

Four Phantoms for General Taylor

It was Elizabeth Hood's ninth birthday, and she was on her way to Fort George one foggy morning with her older sister Kathleen and her parents to deliver some supplies. The British officers at the fort appreciated their business and the fresh food which they provided. However, unbeknown to the Hoods, the British Army had suffered high casualties fighting the Americans at their beachhead landing, earlier in the day. Because the British no longer had enough soldiers left to defend Fort George, they had retreated from Newark.

It seemed too quiet outside the fort palisade as Elizabeth, Kathleen and their parents arrived with a small wagon in tow, later that same morning. There was no guard and the Union Jack was not flying. That's strange, Elizabeth thought to herself. There is no such thing as a fort without a flag.

The mist swirled up from the nearby river and floated over the fort, burying it in a sunken repose. The dim light of morning slowly changed the drab white vapour, from pallid to a phantasmagorical yellow haze. Elizabeth could detect a lingering sense of fear of the unknown.

For a brief moment, she was disorientated. She had no body and could not focus on what had happened to her. The confusion lasted for several minutes, until she was able to look at her mortal body from above. She floated above Fort George and saw the American Army advancing. Below were the damaged bodies of herself, Kathleen and her parents, hit by a stray cannon shot.

A disembodied voice said to her that she should go towards the light. She replied that it was not time to leave and that she had unfinished business at the fort to attend to. That unfinished business would last for the next couple of hundred years. Elizabeth knew that her parents would understand her decision to remain behind on the earth plane. She could be stubborn at the most awkward of times. What Elizabeth didn't expect is to hear was another familiar voice from the past, scolding her for retreating from the light.

"And what my dear gives you the right to overturn the decision of our heavenly hosts," the disembodied voice said.

Elizabeth was quite taken back. "Sorry for the inconvenience. Did I do wrong?" she said.

"Maybe you did and maybe you didn't. But you sure dragged me into it this time," the voice replied.

"Hey, you don't sound like an angel at all," Elizabeth responded.

"Don't you recognize your own sister," the voice queried.

"Kathleen," Elizabeth sounded shocked. "What are you doing here?"

"The same reason you are here. Did you think I got away or something?"

"No, I mean didn't you go with Mother and Father?"

"As you can see, I'm right here," Kathleen replied.

"Well, don't you have to go soon?"

"Not likely and I'm afraid it's your doing my dear."

"Now what have I done?"

"I'm afraid it's what you haven't done. You refused to go to the light. Normally, they would have given you a few days and then maybe tried to bring you up again; however, they felt that you really did mean it."

"That doesn't explain why you're here, does it?" Elizabeth retorted.

"You might say that I wanted to show you the light," Kathleen replied.

"You never could tell a decent joke."

"Never mind the jokes. I want you to understand what you're in for," Kathleen insisted.

"What's the mystery all about?" Elizabeth was getting weary of being bantered about, even if she was a new spirit. "I'm really not ready to go with you, you know."

"I'm afraid you've got that part wrong. I'm going with you," Kathleen insisted. "Listen, Elizabeth. It so happened that I was on my way to the light when I got turned back. They agreed with you that you have some important things to do and that you could use a little help. You might say that you are my heavenly assignment."

"I'm sorry I messed things up for you. Can I help you, by getting them to change their minds?"

"No, this order came directly from the Creator. There is no appeal. I'm afraid this is it. We might as well get started. You got your wish."

"Does that mean that we can stay on earth as long as it takes?" Elizabeth seemed very excited about the prospect of staying near Fort George.

"Yes, I expect that is true. What exactly is it that we are trying to prove anyway? Haven't we done enough already?" Kathleen submitted.

"You mean like getting killed in action while supplying the British troops. Yes, I see what you mean. Don't worry. I'm not going to risk getting trapped in a mirror, a portrait or a bottle. Yes, we must proceed very slowly at first. We don't want to end up haunting some blockhouse. We were meant for greater things."

"What do you really want to do that's so important?" Kathleen asked.

"I think we shall help people. That is what I intend to do."

"Isn't that what we would have done, if we had gone to the light?" Kathleen said.

“It’s not the same thing. We can do what we want to do here. Whatever we do is by choice.”

“I really think the angels would have given us that choice too.” Kathleen sounded concerned.

“Yes, but I would have liked heaven too much. It is better that I do not know how wonderful heaven really is. I’ll find out about heaven soon enough. The Creator has granted me my greatest earthly wish. I intend to follow through.” Elizabeth paused and reflected. “I can promise you one thing Kathleen. From this point onwards, whoever visits Fort George will do so with due respect to the fallen, or they must make amends to the spirit world.”

* * *

Alan and Danny Hood were both hired as student re-enactors at Fort George for the summer. The two boys were natural leaders. Alan was to be promoted to staff sergeant and Danny was promoted to corporal, based on their performances at Fort George and previous summer jobs, at other forts.

Alan had just turned seventeen. He was the size of General Brock himself. Thankfully, he could command his troops like Brock. Alan was very proud of the British involvement in Upper Canada at the time of 1812. His favourite past-time was researching important military events and reading books about the War of 1812.

Danny was three years younger than his brother. He was slim and athletic, and he enjoyed soldiering just like Alan. Together, they would have been regulars in the old British Army.

The summer was just about over before Alan and Danny's parents decided to join them for one last ghost tour. It was arranged that they would have a meal in a local restaurant and then proceed to the ghost tour at Fort George.

It was gloriously warm Saturday in August when their parents arrived at Niagara-on-the-Lake. They headed over to a restaurant which claimed to have a haunted picture of Colonel Butler of Butler's Rangers. The boy's father was interested in the picture and he thought that maybe the boys would be too. Danny made a joke about how the spirits can't be everywhere all of the time.

"Why don't you boys go over talk things over with the Colonel," the boys' father joked. "Perhaps he can give you some tips on army maneuvers."

"Very funny Dad," Danny said, giving his father a funny look. "I don't think you're serious about the portrait Dad; but it looks like we have to go through with it. Come on Alan; let's see what the old Colonel has in mind."

Alan and Danny stood smartly; but walked stiffly towards the portrait of the Colonel. The Colonel's eyes were like beacons that drew them over. Before the boys knew it, they were standing to attention in front of Colonel Butler, commanding officer of Butler's Rangers. Butler's Rangers were famous for their boldness against the enemy during the latter part of the 18th century.

The boys felt a bit foolish at first; then Alan became transfixed by the Colonel's portrait. Danny began to wonder about "what was going on" with Alan, as he looked intently at the portrait. Before the Colonel could wink, Danny was under his spell too. They were both unaware that their father had come up behind them.

"Hey, you two," their father said. He managed to startle them and make them flinch. "I didn't mean to break up your conversation with the Colonel; but I'd rather finish eating here, before it gets too late. We don't want to miss the last call for the ghost tour," their father reminded them.

"Yes, quite so Dad. Sorry about that. The Colonel is quite a mesmerizing chap, isn't he?" Alan said.

"I would say so," Richard said, as he noticed how intently his boys were looking at the Colonel. He couldn't help staring at the portrait himself. "He's a real old timer and a very handsome fellow in that fancy British uniform. Of course, all British Army officers were rather flamboyant in those days, weren't they Mother?" Richard said to Sarah, as he quickly turned around to catch Sarah sneaking up behind him.

"Are you asking my opinion, just because I'm British or are you just making fun of the Colonel?" Sarah retorted, as she felt cheated out of her sneak attack.

"No offence intended. I may be a history professor, but I'm not a know-it-all. I'm sure the Colonel could have told me a thing or two. It's too bad his ghost isn't here to fill me in," Richard suggested.

"Maybe he is Dad. The Colonel is better off here than he is in his rebuilt barracks," Alan replied.

"I'm sure, the Colonel still gets around. Well Colonel, we must go," Richard said, as he saluted the portrait. "Alan, I could almost swear that the portrait winked back at me."

"I can believe it Dad. There's something very queer about the Colonel's portrait," Alan said, as the Hoods joined together and returned to their dining table.

Alan looked a bit drained as he sat down at the table. His father looked up from the roast chicken that had just arrived.

"Hope you enjoy the meal tonight boys. This will be your last night in Niagara-on-the-Lake for the summer," Richard reminded them.

"I'm sorry I forgot to tell you something Dad. Danny and I have to spend another week down here. The job was extended for a special assignment," Alan said, as Danny stared at him in confusion. "Of course we didn't know about it until today; otherwise, we would have told you to come next weekend, so we could have gone home with you.

"Naturally; but it's not a worry, is it Mother?" Sarah agreed. Richard continued, "You boys have certainly learned how to take care of yourselves, and we'd be happy to come back again next weekend and pick you up."

After dinner, as the Hood family were heading towards the restaurant door, Danny took Alan aside.

"Alan, what's the idea of leaving us stranded in Niagara for another week? We don't have any special assignment. Our job here is done."

"Don't worry Danny. We'll be fine. I'll tell you about it, after the ghost tour."

The Hoods arrived at the fort as the long shadows of twilight turned to dusk. The parking lot was still about half full, as they looked for the familiar lantern held by one of the tour guides.

"I think we're too late for the last tour," Danny said. "It's almost dark now and I don't see anyone."

"No look. There's a lantern. That's funny. I didn't see it a minute ago. It looks like there's a small group of people already gathered," Alan added.

The two ghost tour guides were dressed in black cloaks and dark frilly shirts and elaborately decorated tight trousers. Each tour guide held an antique lantern. The tall one looked like a young university student. Her voice was a bit deep for a female. The short one was a young girl around nine years of age. Danny thought it odd that one of the guides was so young.

Alan looked more closely at the older female; but couldn't figure out why he had never seen such an attractive young woman around the fort before. Alan also took the time to look over the rest of the people on the tour. They seemed more like a group that might be going to a Shakespearean play, than a ghost tour. Some of them were wearing capes; others had wide armed frilly shirts with vests. Most of their clothes looked out of time, more like two hundred years ago.

The tour stopped just outside of the fort gates. The usual warnings about the moat were given, but something else more sinister was added. Alan and Danny were both surprised when they thought they heard that they should not speak of ghosts while they were inside the fort.

"That's a strange request for a ghost tour," Alan whispered to Danny. "Perhaps she doesn't want to panic anyone. She must be new to this business."

The Hoods followed the ghost tour to the first blockhouse where the customary ghost tales were to be told, except the tall tour guide stopped short and turned towards Alan.

"A mother and a daughter were blown up here. The mother was trapped in a dimensional warp, where no one can reach her. The daughter's spirit haunts the fort and doesn't know her mother's spirit is trapped between these two buildings forever. Not even the angels can help her," the tour guide said.

"That's weird," Alan said to Danny.

"What's weird?" Danny replied.

"What she just said. Weren't you listening Danny?"

"Listening to what? No one said anything, Alan. What's all the mystery anyway? When are you going to tell me about the Colonel?" Danny asked.

"Not so loud Danny. I don't want Mom and Dad to find out," Alan said in a hushed tone.

"What are you two up to? You sound like you're plotting a conspiracy," Richard said.

"There are no worries here Dad. The tour seems a bit odd tonight; that's all," Danny said.

"Yes, I see what you mean," Richard agreed

After entering the blockhouse, the tall dark haired tour guide motioned everyone to have a seat. The short one was nowhere in sight. No one saw her leave either.

"On some nights, the spirit of a nine-year-old girl can be seen on the stairway, leading to the second floor of the blockhouse. This little girl has been known to join the tour group. The only place she doesn't go is into the tunnel which goes outside the main fort, on the south side. She has been known to tug at peoples' shirts and pull their hair from behind. Still, she is a friendly ghost and will not harm anyone," the tour guide said.

For one split second, Danny thought he saw the short tour guide sitting on the stairs looking directly at him. He blinked and then there was nothing. Voices seemed to be coming out of nowhere. No one else on the tour was paying attention to the conversation. He was getting very edgy. Then he could hear a voice clearly in his mind like it was his own.

"It's Elizabeth, Danny. You used to believe in me. A long time ago, we were friends. Now you've grown up and you don't need me anymore. Danny, I need you to help me. Alan knows what to do. We'll be together soon."

Danny went ice cold. Somewhere in his childhood memory, there was a recollection of the spirit world which intervened on his behalf. Just recently, he doubted, whether it had even happened. But now it was all starting to come back to him. The blockhouse was part of his memory. It seemed familiar and comfortable like he was in another time. The voices he heard now sounded like soldiers going about their barracks duties. Then he heard the tour guide say, it was time to move on towards the tunnel.

After leaving the blockhouse with the crowd, Danny asked Alan if he had heard or seen anything unusual.

"Like a ghost for instance?" Alan said.

"Well, did you see the short tour guide go anywhere?" Danny replied.

"She probably went ahead," Alan suggested. "Maybe, it's past her bedtime. Why? Do you think that she's a ghost Danny?"

"Well, I'm going to ask the tour guide anyway," Danny said, as he walked boldly over to the tall girl. "Excuse me, could you tell me what happened to the little girl that came with you please?"

"There is no little girl on this tour, I should think," the tour guide replied.

"I mean the one that was with you in the parking lot. You know; the one that came into the fort. I didn't see her leave the tour," Danny insisted.

"I think you're mistaken young man. There is no young girl on this tour," the tour guide maintained, as she turned away from Danny.

Danny was mystified. He followed the tour group around the fort, not realizing where he was going. The little girl's image preyed on his mind. He could no longer keep his thoughts to himself.

"Alan, she's a ghost. She looked directly at me from the stairs in the blockhouse and then told me that you knew what to do. Alan, can't you tell me what's going to happen next?" Danny pleaded.

"We're going to Butler's Barracks after Mom and Dad leave. That's all I know Danny. It's important. We'll find out what's going on when we get there."

The tour group followed the guide outside of the fort for the ghost tour debriefing.

"If anyone saw anything unusual on this tour and you want to share it with the group, now is the time," the tour guide said.

The group seemed to melt away in every direction at that point. The Hoods never saw anyone leave. They just vanished like the little girl.

"I hope you enjoyed the tour," the tour guide said with an impish smile, as she looked directly at Alan. Her dark eyes seem to look right through him. "The last time I did this tour, there were over thirty soldiers waiting outside the fort for the group to exit. One of them tried to attach himself to a tourist; however, that got sorted out and they all decided to stay at the fort where they belong."

Alan felt a bit embarrassed. Richard and Sarah looked at each other like they were anxious to leave. It would be midnight soon and they had a long drive back to their hometown.

"Thanks for the tour." Richard began, as he turned to shake hands with the tour guide. Then he stopped in his tracks looking like he had dropped his wallet. "Hey, where did she go?"

"Everyone's gone Richard. I wouldn't worry too much about it. It's a bit too spooky tonight, if you ask me," Sarah commented.

"You boys will be off to bed then. Your mother and I will see you next Saturday," Richard said.

"Take care Mom and Dad. Have a good journey. We'll be fine. Come along Danny. Let's head back to our other home."

The boys started walking beyond the parking lot. They turned around one last time to wave at their parents, as they drove away. At that moment, Danny almost believed that his parents had deserted him.

"I can see the barracks from here Danny. We're almost there," Alan exclaimed, as he tried to cheer Danny up.

"That's not what I'm worried about," Danny replied, in a nervous voice, as he pointed towards the monk like silhouette. Danny forgot about being homesick, when he realized the shadow standing in the dark was watching them. "Alan, there's someone there waiting for us."

"It's you, from the ghost tour at the fort," Danny said, to the little girl.

"Yes, it is Danny," the short tour guide said, as she stepped out of the darkness and lit her lantern.

"Hey, how do you know my name?" Danny said.

"That's simply enough. But right now, you want to know why you're here," she said.

"Are you working for Colonel Butler too?" Alan asked.

"In a way, we are looking for the same thing. The only difference is that I can help you. The Colonel has some influence; but he can't assist you," she said.

"What's your name, since you already know ours," Alan asked.

"It's Elizabeth. You should have listened to your little brother," she said, with a grin.

"Do you know anything about the ghosts at Fort George?" Danny asked.

"I can't explain everything right now Danny because there isn't enough time. It's almost midnight and its very dangerous being around here. People have been known to disappear from Butler's Barracks at this time of the night."

"Then don't you think it might be a better idea to move away from the Colonel's old haunt. Maybe the old gentleman is behind all the disappearances," Alan suggested.

"In a way he is. But he's not responsible for the problems," Elizabeth said.

"It sounds like the Colonel needs some help," Alan said.

"Yes Alan. The Colonel recognized you as a kindred spirit at the restaurant. He believes that you and Danny can perform a feat that no one before you has been successful in doing. That way people will stop disappearing into the past," she said.

"That sounds easy. What do we have to do," Alan said to humour her, since he really didn't believe her story.

"Well, I'm afraid you must risk going into the past. But you shouldn't worry. I'll be there with you."

"Let me ask you a big question Elizabeth," Danny said, taking her a little more seriously. "Did any of those people who disappeared, ever come back?"

"No. I'm afraid not. Some of their gravestones started showing up in the local graveyard. Their names started showing up in the records too. A few of them were soldiers like you, who ended up fighting against the Americans during the War of 1812."

"So, what happens when you go back in time in your modern clothes?" Danny asked.

"You will be dressed in the clothes that you would have worn had you lived in the past. If you're lucky enough to return to the present, you will return in your regular clothes."

"How long do you expect us to stay in the past Elizabeth?" Danny asked.

"That's the main problem. If you don't succeed, then you must remain there. You normally have a week to accomplish everything."

"That doesn't sound like good odds to me. I don't think I should commit my future to a gamble. Sorry Elizabeth, but we may not be the soldiers you're looking for," Alan said.

"Oh, but you are. You did live during the War of 1812 in your previous lives. Alan you were General Brock and Danny, you were Captain FitzGibbon a daring, debonair officer of the Bully Boys Regiment. Brock will already have passed on to the afterlife, so there is no danger of meeting him. However,

Danny must not meet FitzGibbon; otherwise there is a chance that he may be stuck in the 19th century for the duration."

"Well, that's just about enough for me. Come on Danny, are you coming with me? Sorry Elizabeth, but we've got to get ready for school this fall. I need to get good marks this year. It's getting tougher to get into university," Alan said.

"You mean you didn't notice," she said.

"Notice what?" Alan replied.

"Why, we're in the 19th century silly. As soon as you move off this picnic table, it will be December of 1813. You'll be dressed for a very cold winter's night. Don't move until you're ready."

"Okay, your bluff worked. What are we looking for Elizabeth?" Alan asked.

"A chess set," she replied.

"Is that all?" Alan asked.

"This is a very special chess set," she said.

"Oh, I think Danny and I can handle the job," Alan said.

"It belongs to the American commander and you will have to swap it with Butler's chess set. We will arrive close to Colonel Butler's cabin, in the year 1813; but we must visit his hideaway first. You'll have to return to Butler's cabin within a week's time. The worst case is when they only give you one day to finish your task."

"Do we have any choice?" Alan asked.

"Not anymore," Elizabeth said.

"Do we have any hope of completing the job?"

"With my help, you might."

“Well, I’m going to see if you’re telling a fib right now. Come on Danny get off the picnic table. It doesn’t look like 1813 to me,” Alan said.

As soon as Alan jumped from the picnic table, it seemed to disappear. He felt a terrific cold wind. It was almost pitch dark and he could barely see through a blowing snow shower. He was wearing a thick, heavy coat made of bear fur. He was also wearing thick hairy boots that worked like snowshoes on the soft parts of the ground. His great furry mitts seemed to reach for the ground. But it was the enormous beaver hat on his head that made him look most impressive.

The recent light snow eddied up in little wind currents; then blew away, over the icy snow crusts, with a few strong gusts of wind. Fortunately, the snow on the ground was hard packed and easy to walk upon. Even though the fur coats that the boys were wearing repelled the elements, the sound of the wind as lonely and forlorn as a graveyard, sent chills to their very souls.

“Danny, Elizabeth, where are you?” Alan shouted, his words being eaten up by the biting wind.

“Right behind you silly,” Elizabeth said. “One thing Alan, and you too Danny; no one can see me, except you two.”

“What do you mean Elizabeth? You mean; you mean,” Danny said.

“Yes, Danny. I’m a ghost.”

“That’s no surprise,” Alan remarked, as he pulled his thick bear fur collar around his neck. “It looks like we really did go back in time. It feels more like the Ice Age; than 1813. I expect they didn’t have global warming. You’re not joking about any of this, are you Elizabeth?”

“In fact, you will find that no one “jokes around” here. Danny you must be careful to avoid FitzGibbon. The good news is that the spirits of Butler’s Rangers will try and help you. The bad news is that FitzGibbon could interfere; since he is on a separate mission and is expected to be near the same location.

You will have to penetrate the American lines and take some chances. If you fail, at best, you will be stuck in the past. At worst, you will be shot as spies. Both of you must go. I would rather that Danny didn't make this trip because of the additional risks; but there is no choice. Both of you are needed to increase the power of the chess set."

"Elizabeth, what will happen in the future, if we fail?" Alan said.

"It may be difficult for you to understand this, but the balance of things will be upset. The American soldiers could become more evil in their pursuit of victory at any cost. For example, they may stay in Upper Canada during the winter and fight, instead of retreating across the border like they normally do at this time of the year. Many historical events and situations could be altered by virtue of the Americans staying."

"Are you sure you're only nine years old?" Danny said.

"I look nine years old; but I'm not really. I'm not like all the other ghosts. The Creator wanted me to help you. I've waited almost two hundred years for the opportunity to set things right. Now here is the rest of the story. There was an additional chess set that was left at Fort George at the time of the War of 1812 which belonged to Colonel Butler. In the Colonel's will, the chess set was to remain with the British Army. A few older soldiers, who had served with Colonel Butler's Rangers, took the chess set to Fort George initially. The chess set had been moved by the spirits from the fort during the American invasion in order to safeguard it. Two American soldiers found it at a home in Newark, before the town was burnt down and played a game of chess in which the British side lost. Butler's chess set must be found and brought back to the future, in order that the spirits of the game can be balanced. Do you have any questions so far?" Elizabeth asked.

"Can you tell us a bit more about Butler's chess set, Elizabeth?" Alan replied.

"Butler's chess set ended up in the hands of an American millionaire. He donated the set to the fort on the condition that no earthly hand should change the American checkmate. The set is in a tamper-proof glass container. As such, the chess set pieces cannot be moved by mortal hands. The millionaire had plenty of bad luck, after he acquired it. He couldn't wait to donate it. Apparently, the chess set must never leave the fort. Also, the fort is to be commanded by evil spirits on the two hundredth anniversary of the War of 1812, unless the British soldier spirits, who are in checkmate, can reverse their positions. Since no mortal can move the chess set pieces; the spirits of the chess set must have enough power to accomplish their task. Only the spirits of British soldiers, in particular Butler's Rangers, can do the job. However, mortal intervention is still required. The Colonel has been searching for the chosen ones for almost two hundred years and it looks like he has found them in you two."

"I don't pretend to understand a lot of this spiritual business Elizabeth. But we must not fail for our own sake," Danny said.

"There one other problem and I'm afraid you're not going to like it," Elizabeth said.

"You didn't give us the good news first," Alan said.

"There isn't any good news concerning this mission. There is a curse on the chess set for anyone who has anything to do with altering it."

"And now for the bad news," Alan said.

"You made a few enemies back in this time Alan. They haven't forgotten you. They haven't forgotten you either Danny. If you succeed in bringing Colonel Butler's chess set back to the present, every evil spirit who had anything to do with the curse, will follow you to the present and haunt you until you go mad."

"I'm a little confused about this chess set business; but if we don't get out this place, we're going to be frozen before we even see an American soldier or an evil spirit," Danny said.

"Before we go any further, you might have forgotten that the Americans control Newark. You are basically spies in civilian clothing, since this is occupied territory. I suggest we proceed with caution. I know a place where we can stay for a few days, before we grab the chess set," Elizabeth said.

"No problem," Danny said, without fully understanding their situation. "Honestly Elizabeth, don't you feel the cold at all. You only have enough clothes on for a summer's evening."

"Silly. I'm a ghost."

"Oh yes. I forgot."

"Follow me. We haven't got far to go," she said.

"Look Alan. Elizabeth isn't making any footprints."

"Just remember not to talk to me around anyone. They may think you're very odd. In fact, they will think you're quite mad," Elizabeth answered.

"Yes, I know that one. You keep reminding me. If I wasn't freezing to death, I would have said I was dreaming," Danny said, as his curious questions were put aside in favor of tightening the ear muffs on his fur hat.

"Don't worry Danny. You have some money in your pocket, if you need it and you will be able to get a nice hot drink and a good meal in no time. The best place to go is about three miles from here. No American soldiers will find you there," Elizabeth reassured Danny.

"And what if they do find us?" Alan said.

"That's where I come in. Just leave it to me," Elizabeth postulated, as they approached their destination, after more than an hour of strenuous hiking.

In front of them was a dwelling. It seemed to come out of nowhere. The thick black clouds that hid the moon that night didn't help. Besides feeling lost, Danny had another thought that Elizabeth might desert them.

“For a minute, I thought you left us here in 1813 to defend ourselves,” Danny said, as he heard the swaying of tree branches in front of the cabin. His relief turned to panic, as the snowy evergreen branches swung at him, causing snow to fly down the back of his neck. The small sharp needles on the branches lifted his fur hat, right off of his head.

“Colonel Butler use to come to this log cabin on occasion to get away from it all. In fact, some of his belongings are still here,” Elizabeth said calmly, as she lit a lantern. She looked up and noticed that Danny was dancing in step with the waving tree branches. “Whatever happened to you Danny? Your face is covered in snow.”

“Whatever happened to me? Whatever happened to you? I think you walked right through that large evergreen tree and left the snow for me to clear. Honestly Elizabeth, I couldn’t see a thing. I swear that you disappeared right in front of me,” Danny said, as he looked at her in amazement.

“I’m really sorry Danny. I was preoccupied. I’ll explain everything in a minute,” Elizabeth said, as she cleared the snow from the bottom of the front door.

“Oh dear, oh dear me; I’ve made a miscalculation,” Elizabeth said as she entered the cabin.

“You’re telling me. There are enough rocks, trees and slopes around here to discourage any visitor. Are you sure we have the right place?” Alan said, as he shook some snow from his mitts.

“No, you don’t understand. It just occurred to me. This is the night,” Elizabeth exclaimed.

“Yes, we know. This is the night we arrived in 1813,” Alan replied.

“No. This is the night that the American General is secretly plotting to burn Newark. That’s why he removed all of his belongings and his chess set from Fort George and took them to Fort Niagara.”

"Does that mean we have to return to Fort Niagara?" Alan cried, as if someone had thrown ice cold water at him.

"You mean we've just walked three miles and now we have to walk three miles back, cross the river and steal the General's chess set right from under his nose," Danny added.

"You both are silly billies, aren't you? Have you forgotten what I told you? The Colonel's chess set is located at a cabin near Fort George. Don't you remember what I said about the two American soldiers who found it? Now that we possess the American General's chess set, you must swap the two sets before the town is burnt down. The General's chess set that we currently possess, must be returned to him, before he captures the Colonel's set. I will help you."

"Now, I know I'm mad," Danny said, as he stood in disbelief before Elizabeth. "You say that you've just stolen an American General's chess set; then I'm going to return it to him before he burns Newark to the ground. Why don't I just hand him the blindfold that he's going to put over my eyes, before he puts me in front of a firing squad. Honestly, Elizabeth, I can't believe you anymore," Danny said.

"Yes, you can silly. Look at the table in front of you."

On the large, oak table was a beautiful chess set of American and British soldiers, based on the American War of Independence.

"The Colonel sure has good tastes," Alan said as he admired the fancy chess set. I'm glad you changed your mind and decided to swap them for us."

"That's not the Colonel's chess set," Elizabeth said.

"I'm confused again. Now, there's a third chess set," Danny said.

"You two have a lot to learn. You just don't get it. I took the General's chess set when he wasn't looking."

"Yes, I believe you," Danny agreed, until bewilderment set in. "But you've been here all the time, haven't you?"

"Remember when you thought I had left you. Well, I did actually and I put the American General's chess set in the fourth dimension. I wasn't sure if I had enough power to fight the evil spirits and bring the chess set here to this cabin. I knew you would have trouble getting the General's chess set and I did my best. Even though I've saved you the trouble of crossing the river, there is one thing I cannot do. I cannot bring the Colonel's chess set back to the present. The two of you must do that. There is still a real danger," Elizabeth explained.

"Since you've spoiled the General's game of chess, the General will have better things to do," Alan said.

"Like burning Newark to the ground," Danny added.

"We must get something to eat and make our way back to Newark with the General's chess set," Elizabeth said, as she paused and looked outside. "It looks like the snow is beginning to drift in here and that might slow us down." Elizabeth turned from the window and looked directly at the boys. "Danny and Alan, we must be near Butler's other cabin by twelve o'clock midnight with the Colonel's chess set in our possession, or his hideaway log cabin will be your new home." Elizabeth thought it might be better build up the boys' resilience after losing some of it along the way. "I know you two don't feel like eating, but you're going to need your strength before we head out. I brought some nice mutton and vegetables from the General's stores which I found near the chess set. This should be quite a celebration."

"Don't think we're not grateful Elizabeth. You're performed enough miracles for a lifetime. Without you, we wouldn't stand a chance. It's better to have the spirits on our side," Danny said.

“Maybe you’d better thank me later Danny. There are two American officers who are playing chess right now at Butler’s other cabin. We must swap the sets without them knowing it.”

“That should be easy for you Elizabeth. Just do it,” Alan said.

“Not quite. Remember it’s your task. Once you’ve completed the trade, you will be returned to your time, at midnight. It looks like we have just enough time, so we’d better get started.”

After a hasty, but hearty meal of roast chicken and stew, they retraced their steps back to the future site of Butler’s Barracks.

They spotted the cabin they were seeking near Fort George, after almost two hours of heavy slogging, through the fresh fallen snow. Within Butler’s cabin, there was a trap door which led to a shallow basement. In the basement, there were two American officers playing a game of chess. They appeared to be pleased with their find.

“I think I’ve got you Captain, sir,” the thin Lieutenant said. “That will teach you to take the side of the British.

“Yes Lieutenant. I lost the draw on that one for sure. Someone had to take the losing side. This chess set is good enough for a general. We’ll have to take the chess set with us. General Taylor might give us an easy duty for this prize,” the Captain said. “Did you hear something upstairs Lieutenant? Grab your pistol. Let’s have a look see.”

The two tense officers peeped out of the slit in the trapdoor; but couldn’t see anything from their vantage point; so they decided to scramble into the upper cabin with their pistols in hand. The Lieutenant was too close to the Captain. He tripped. The Lieutenant’s weapon was discharged, as it fell onto the hardwood floor. A small ball of lead hit the front door with a thud.

“Be careful, you clumsy clod. How in blue blazes did they ever make a soldier out of you, never mind an officer?” Captain Black asked.

“Sorry sir. These army boots that I’m wearing are two sizes too large. They’re great for guard duty, when you need the extra two pairs of socks to keep your feet warm; but these boots are no good for climbing ladders sir,” the Lieutenant said, as Captain Black shook his head in disgust.

Elizabeth stood in front of Danny and Alan while the American officers searched the main floor of the cabin. She made herself and the boys invisible to the American soldiers. The soldiers left the cabin and continued to search outside for intruders.

“Quick. Go down the ladder, through the trapdoor and grab the Colonel’s chess set,” Elizabeth said.

“Won’t they notice anything?” Danny asked.

“No. I will fool them. They will see the original set until midnight; then it will revert to the American General’s War of Independence set.”

“Elizabeth, they’re back already. We’re trapped,” Alan said, as he gathered up Colonel Butler’s chess set.

“No, we’re not. The General has arrived,” Elizabeth said, as she put the General’s chess set on the table.

There was a loud knocking at the door. The General’s party stood outside and demanded to find out why the two officers had not taken up their offensive positions in Newark. The Captain stated that they had some important information to go over. He even found a rare and beautiful chess set which was based on the War of Independence. He thought it would make a great present for the General’s collection. The General appeared to soften a bit. The Captain made his way down the ladder in a hurry before the General changed his mind about disciplining the two delinquent officers. Elizabeth made the boys invisible again to the Captain's eyes, as the Captain quickly gathered up the chess set in a canvas bag.

Danny and Alan could both hear the Captain presenting the chess set to the General. If that chess set was to revert to its original form too soon, perhaps they would search the cabin for the other set. They could only wait.

"What in blue blazes? This is an outrage! Why, this is my chess set. It disappeared from Fort Niagara this very night. If this is a joke, you two will be spending your time doing sentry duty, without the benefit of a chess set," the General said.

"Yes sir, I mean no sir. This is no joke sir. We recovered the chess set for you," the quick thinking Captain said. "We didn't get a chance to check the stores below for any other evidence of contraband, did we Lieutenant?"

The Lieutenant's jaw had dropped and it continued to drop until the Captain grabbed him and pulled him towards the ladder. After making their way down the ladder, they saw the three ghostly figures standing there. There was a little girl in white and two British soldiers. One was a general in a red tunic and the other was a lieutenant in a green tunic. The American Lieutenant felt faint as the figures glowed for an instance and just disappeared. Both American officers climbed back up the ladder, as fast as they could.

"It was General Brock sir. He's come back from the dead to fight us. It's not a good omen sir. We should make haste of it," the Captain said.

"With a militia officer, who is afraid of his own shadow, we should make haste and retreat and not so much as lift a finger. I say, burn the town down Captain Black and pull back across the river, as soon as you're done. Don't take any longer than necessary, or you will be facing a court martial. If you so much as mention anything about this General Brock's ghost nonsense to anyone, I will have you shot at sunrise. Do I make myself clear Captain?"

"Yes sir. Very clear sir," the Captain replied.

“Then, what are you waiting for, you bumbling fool. Burn the town down now!”

“What was he so scared of Elizabeth? Could he see right through you or something?” Alan asked.

“No I’m afraid he could see right through all of us. You might say that your appearance changed a bit when you left your time and went back into the past. You appeared as General Brock to him. Brock could be intimidating, if you were right up close to him. It’s too bad your father didn’t make the trip. He would have been General Tecumseh, the great Shawnee chief. Even the American General would have run for his life, rather than face Tecumseh’s tomahawk. Either Brock or Tecumseh could have saved Newark from the torch; however, that was not to be. Your timely intervention did save a few lives. Some American soldiers heard about General Brock’s ghost and decided to leave town. They believed that they would be haunted, if they stayed in Upper Canada, with the General’s spirit still in the area.”

“I guess we made it back okay, right Elizabeth?” Danny said.

“As soon as you move, we will be back at Butler’s Barracks. You will be in your regular clothes, as you were, before you left. Also, the chess set at Fort George went back to the past with you. It’s now back in the present, at Fort George and the British have the checkmate on the American soldiers. That should prevent any further problems related to the curse. There’s just one problem though.”

“I hope we don’t have to go through this again Elizabeth,” Danny pleaded.

“Silly. You forgot again, didn’t you Danny. The evil spirits from the past have followed you to the present and joined other evil armies. I’m afraid it’s going to take awhile to get rid of them. Your father is not going to be pleased either. He’s going to need the Council’s help.”

“What is the Council all about?” Alan said.

"The Senior Council of Angels of course. This job is too big for me now. It's much bigger than I bargained for. You, Danny and your father will have to defeat the evil armies with the Council's help. The curse is upon you."

Alan and Danny returned to their lodging in Niagara-on-the- Lake. Both of them felt rather dejected and exhausted from their ordeal. They soon fell into a deep sleep. Their dreams were encounters in the spirit world. Their visions foretold what problems the Hood family could expect by Halloween, if certain events were to unfold as predicted, assuming that Alan and Danny were to do nothing about the evil spirits that had followed them back from the past.

Both boys were sound asleep when every mirror in the room flew off the wall and came down in a terrific crash. The boys woke up terrified.

"What happened?" Danny asked, as he jumped from his bed.

"It's an angel from the Senior Council, an angel without a name. He wants us to return to the fort tonight. We have another mission. If we don't return to the past, we will be haunted forever. Did you have a dream about Dad being attacked by a demon?" Alan asked Danny.

"Yes, it was terrifying. The demon almost got him too."

"That was no dream. All the things that you dreamed about will take place, if we don't do something to stop the evil armies."

"Are you sure there is no other way Alan?"

"No Danny. This is a directive from the highest authority. We must return to the fort and receive our instructions."

Alan and Danny returned to the Fort George ghost tour the following evening. They figured that it would be easier to meet Elizabeth at night.

Dusk was falling around them, as they reached the entrance to the parking lot at Fort George. The ghost tour group was beginning to assemble at the far end of the parking lot. The boys walked over to the guide holding the lit lantern and paid for two admissions. They were disappointed to see that Elizabeth and her sister were not part of the ceremonies.

"I hope this works out," Alan said, as he paid for their admissions. "There's no sign of her."

"It's still early and it's a full moon tonight," Danny reminded him. "I think that Elizabeth already knows we're here. I'm sure she knows about our dream as well."

As Danny looked towards the darkening fort, he thought he could see two black hooded capes heading towards the fort. Neither of them appeared to be with a ghost tour.

"Do you see that?" Danny said.

"See what Danny?" Alan replied.

"There were two cloaked figures headed to the fort a minute ago. I swear it."

"I believe you Danny. It could have been our friends. Then again, it could have been those evil spirits that were sent to haunt us. Perhaps, it was not such a great idea to come back here tonight."

"The only other place we could have tried to contact Elizabeth is Butler's Barracks. I'm sure you don't want to go back there again either," Danny said.

"Something tells me that is exactly where we are going, after the ghost tour. Colonel Butler isn't finished with us yet," Alan said.

The ghost tour went without incident and without Elizabeth; but Danny wasn't about to give up on her.

"It's almost midnight. Let's go to Butler's Barracks. Perhaps, Elizabeth will show up there," Danny said.

"I think we dreamed this whole thing up Danny," Alan said. "We might have been conned. What if Elizabeth doesn't exist? Why would a ghost wait two hundred years for us to turn up?"

"Maybe we got it wrong and she's the one who is doing us a favor," Danny said, as they reached the darkened lot of Butler's Barracks.

"What took you two? I've been waiting here for almost an hour. It's almost midnight. The evil spirits will be here soon," said the dark hooded, cloaked figure.

"Elizabeth is that you?" Danny said.

"Silly, of course it's me. I hope you enjoyed your little vacation back here. It's time for us to return to the past," she said.

"So that angel dream was no dream," Alan said.

"In fact, it was a dream. Dreams are interactions with the spirit world. However, dreams serve different purposes. Your dream was a warning. The angel gave you a premonition of what could be; so that you could be forewarned and forearmed. Too many evil spirits came back with us. They are beginning to change the future. The only problem is that we must return to the past for about five days this time and I'm sorry to say that we need that other chess set that we left behind after all. It became too evil, after we took the Colonel's chess set. You will appear in the cellar again, where you barely escaped before. You will be captured this time and taken to Fort Niagara, where the American soldiers intend to shoot you. Instead, you will need to return to Butler's Barracks by next Saturday at daybreak, or you will be lost to the past forever. I believe that both of your gravestones are in a cemetery near here already. Your chances of survival are slim."

"Do we have any choice?" Alan asked.

"Would you rather be haunted forever?" Elizabeth replied.

“If you would just sit over on this picnic table beside me, I have something else to tell you,” Elizabeth said. “Do you remember my older sister that did the ghost tour the other day? Well, the Senior Council of Angels decided that the job was too big. She’s been called back for now. They’ve appointed a very important angel instead. He’s been sent here to help all of us. He’s trying to stay in the background as much as possible. In fact, he wants to be known as the angel without a name. He will answer to angel, since no spirit has that name.”

“What do we need protection from exactly?” Alan asked.

“Thanks for reminding me about the evil spirits. I think they’re here already. It fact, it’s done.”

“What’s done Elizabeth?” Alan asked, looking bewildered.

“Oh nothing, just stay where you are for a little bit longer. We’ve been transported back again you know. When you get off this picnic table, you will be back in 1813.”

“Do you have any idea what is going to happen, Elizabeth?” Alan said.

“Yes, I’m afraid you will be arrested on the spot. Alan you may even be shot for wearing General Brock’s uniform. I don’t know how that happened. There must have been a time slip.”

“Well, if you have to get shot for something, something else doesn’t matter, does it?” Alan quibbled. “Besides General Brock was killed at Queenston Heights before Newark was invaded. What am I going to be charged with: robbing graves?”

Alan got excited and jumped off the picnic table, before anyone could stop him. In an instant, he was back in that same cellar with the American General, the Captain and the Lieutenant pointing their pistols at him.

“Maybe they tried to escape through a secret passage,” the startled American General said to the Captain and the Lieutenant, as he looked closer at Alan.

"Come out where I can see you. You're a bit young to be a general soldier boy. Where did you hide your fancy uniform?"

Alan was just as startled to find Elizabeth still standing beside him, but there was no mention of the little girl ghost.

"Come on then. Speak up man. My officers are nervous enough about ghosts and spirits, without British generals popping out of nowhere and chess sets that turn into different sorts," the American General added.

"It's a long story General. We thought you'd be pleased to get your chess set back," Alan said.

"Is this some kind of a joke? I left my chess set at Fort Niagara. What do you know about it and what is my set doing here?"

"That's a very long story General. Perhaps the Captain and the Lieutenant are right about seeing ghosts. There have been some sighted lately," Alan replied.

"Take these two to the fort Captain Black. They both look mad to me. Maybe they've been hiding in this cellar too long."

"For your information, there's a ghost right beside you General," Danny said, as he became more annoyed with the arrogant General.

"No tricks or I'll have you both shot on the spot," the Captain warned them.

"Elizabeth, why don't you blow out the General's lantern?" Danny continued.

Elizabeth just shook her head.

"Danny and Alan, you must both go to Fort Niagara. There are too many soldiers nearby and we can't escape for a few days. You must get that chess set back from the General and be back here within the week. I'll see you at the fort after you arrive."

Well, smart guy. Where is the ghost that you promised?" the Lieutenant said.

"Oh, I'm afraid she's busy right now; but she's going to meet us at Fort Niagara later on. That's where we're going isn't it?" Danny said.

"General, we're wasting our time with these two fools. Why don't we shoot them now, or send them to a loony-bin?" the Lieutenant said.

"Maybe I'm loony too. All this ghost nonsense from you and Captain Black is getting on my nerves. Now there are British soldiers who claim to have ghostly allies. Well, they can meet their ghost friend in the fort's prison. I'd still like to look further into this chess set lunacy," the General said.

"Danny, before I go, you should tell the General that he will find his chess set at Fort Niagara," Elizabeth said. "Tell the General that the ghost put it back for him and that the Captain was mistaken. He should look a bit closer at the one that he now has."

"That's crazy. Are you sure Elizabeth?"

"Who are you talking with soldier?" the Captain said.

"I was talking to the ghost. She's gone now, but she wanted me to tell the General that his chess set is back at Fort Niagara," Danny said.

"I'm beginning to feel like a lunatic myself. We never should have tried to burn Newark on the night of the full moon. Let's see that set again Captain Black," the American General said, as he opened the canvas bag and examined each of the chess set pieces. "This is a War of Independence set like mine; but it's not a new set. Who do you think these green-coated soldiers are Captain Black?"

"Why I believe they are Butler's Rangers sir."

"Come on you two. Get ready to move," the Lieutenant said, as he prodded the two prisoners with his long pistol. "General Taylor, I'd like to personally request permission to escort these two prisoners to Fort Niagara."

"Granted; but be sure to go downstream from the lake far enough, where the ice is thicker," the General warned him.

“It will be a mistake to torch Newark sir,” Alan said, to the General. “Why don’t you just leave the town alone?”

“Spoken like a British soldier, I’m sure,” the Lieutenant said.

“Just a minute Lieutenant; let’s hear what our clever friend has to say. Why is it a mistake lad?” the American General asked.

“Nothing sir; it’s just not a good idea to destroy the town.” Alan thought twice about telling the truth, since that could cause problems for them. If he tried to change history, then he would be stuck in the past. “It just doesn’t seem right to attack civilians. That’s all sir,” Alan added, thinking that he had said enough.

“Yes, I see your point lad; but I must teach the British a lesson in manners before we depart; then they won’t be so anxious to invade our country.”

The General could not be further from the truth. The burning of Newark would be one of the biggest mistakes that the Americans would make during the War of 1812. If this General had been regular army; then he probably would not have made the mistake of burning out the civilians. The Americans would pay a high price because of this General’s ignorance of human nature. There would be many revenge attacks and burning incidents, from Buffalo to the American President’s place of residence.

“Lieutenant, take these two to the fort immediately with an armed escort,” the General commanded.

The General paused and took a deep breath, before delivering his final blow.

“I want every free standing structure burnt to the ground. The British will not attack us this winter. They will be too busy building log cabins to live in,” the General said, satisfied that he could clear out of Upper Canada for the winter and find more comfortable lodgings in America where he wouldn’t be harassed by marauding British troops and Indians. It was no place for a gentleman like himself.

The night was cold and crisp as the American soldiers and their two prisoners crossed the Niagara River. The Lieutenant and two other soldiers that accompanied the boys had not gone upstream far enough, before crossing the river. The cracking of ice under their combined weight was a warning.

"Lieutenant, this is suicide. We're too close together for this thin ice. Where did you say you came from?" Alan asked.

"I'm from Kentucky, soldier boy and if anyone is going to go through the ice, it will be you because I've got Old Bessie trained right on you. If Old Bessie doesn't get you boy, then my Old Bayonet will."

"Your Old Bayonet nothing," Alan replied, as the piercing sound from a large crack in the ice, alerted the boys to take action. Then, the water rushed in.

"Run Danny. Run," Alan shouted.

There was a terrific boom behind them as one of the American soldiers slipped on the wet ice and accidentally discharged his weapon. The soldiers retreated back to shore; whereas the boys managed to get past the wet spot onto more solid ice and make it across to the American side.

"Keep going Danny. They'll be following us soon enough," Alan said.

"Where do you two think you're going?" the disembodied voice said.

"Put your hands up Alan. There's no use in it," Danny said.

"Silly. I asked you where do you think you're going and you put your hands up."

"Elizabeth. What are you doing here? I thought you went to Fort Niagara," Danny said.

“That’s right. I was waiting for you at the fort. Now I find that you’ve managed to escape. This could be awkward.”

“Why do we have to go to a miserable cold and damp fort, just to go to jail?” Danny said. “Why don’t you just grab the chess set and we’ll be on our way.”

“Danny, I told you before; you have to remain in this area for about a week. I thought it would be safer to remain in jail. Instead you want to escape and do what: hide in the woods? Perhaps you would like to join the British assault on the fort or would you prefer to be rescued and released? Now you’ve complicated everything. You are also taking too many risks. What are we going to do now?”

“I’ve got an idea Elizabeth. If you can get us some uniforms from Fort Niagara, we can join the American Militia. They’ll be happy take us on at the fort.” Alan suggested.

“What’s going to happen when the assault takes place later this week? The British don’t know us,” Danny objected.

“That’s the chance we’ll have to take. Elizabeth could you help us to get some American uniforms that fit?” Alan asked.

“It’s a good idea Alan. But I don’t like it. You will be in real danger from the British in a few days time,” Elizabeth warned him.

“Yes, but it will also be easier to grab the chess set as Americans,” Alan said.

“A chess set,” Danny said. “Is that all you’re concerned about?”

“Isn’t that what we came here for?” Alan said. “I would rather not be locked up either. That is not so appealing.”

“Listen, Alan. A British attack is not very appealing either. The British took the Americans by surprise at Fort Niagara and they used their bayonets, or did you forget that?”

"No, I didn't forget. In fact, I'm working on an action plan right now."

"I think this General Brock stuff is going to your head Alan. Well, you'd better work fast; I can hear something coming through the bush behind us. I have a feeling that we've on our way to Fort Niagara either way," Danny said.

"Hold it where you are."

"Not again," Danny whispered.

The three American soldiers surrounded them with their muskets.

"Speak and identify yourselves," the Lieutenant said. The Lieutenant looked at them a bit closer. "You two shouldn't be so close to the river at this time of night. You could have been shot as spies. Where did you come from?"

Alan felt helpless, until he realized that he was wearing an American Militia uniform. Danny realized he was in a different uniform, as he tripped over two muskets which were leaning beside a tree, next to him.

"We thought we heard noises here a minute ago; so we hid here, beside this tree. We thought we might track them down. When we heard American voices, we put our muskets down," Alan said.

"Well, we're looking for two prisoners. They look similar to you, except they were wearing civilian clothes. They also tried to trick me into believing that General Brock was still alive. Maybe the British plan to surround us with generals and ghosts," the Lieutenant said.

"That's real funny Lieutenant," one of the soldiers said. "Can you imagine an army of British generals attacking us?"

"Shut up, you fool. They could be standing right behind us," the Lieutenant said to the soldier. The soldier turned sharply to look for an ambush with a glint in his eye. His musket almost knocked the Lieutenant over. "Fool. You almost knocked my block off, you gaping big idiot."

"Sorry sir," was all the soldier could mumble.

The Lieutenant began to realize that everyone had stopped to look at him like he was a lunatic. Perhaps, he really was starting to go mad. It was time he started to act like an officer in the American Army.

"Your musket is useless anyway soldier, after you dropped it on the wet ice. We'd better get back to the fort in case there are British troops following us. Even if there are no enemy troops around, we'll freeze to death here." Then he turned from his two soldiers and looked closer at the two boys. "We got our feet wet back there on that river," the Lieutenant explained, as he pointed towards the river.

"Yes, we should be getting back to the fort Lieutenant," Alan agreed.

"Where did you two boys say you were from?" the Lieutenant asked.

"We didn't say Lieutenant; but we're from Buffalo. We heard you needed extra help up here," Alan added.

"Oh, is that what your heard? Then you haven't been across the border yet."

"No sir. We've just joined," Danny said.

"Well, you don't sound like Americans to me," the Lieutenant said. Then he pulled his musket up sharply like he was going to shoot them. "I'm going to keep my eye on you two; so don't try anything funny. Just remember, Old Bessie here doesn't like any surprises."

In the cold and bitter air, there was an acrid smell of burning wood, as Newark was torched. The boys had a good view of the shimmering orange-red horizon that was once Newark, as they walked unchallenged, up the path to Fort Niagara. As Danny and Alan passed through the fortified walls of Fort Niagara, the Lieutenant ordered his soldiers to arrest them.

"You two didn't fool me for a minute. How did you manage to get changed into those uniforms after you left the river?" the Lieutenant asked his prisoners, once they were surrounded by a dozen blue and grey, uniformed soldiers. The boys looked down at the ground, tight lipped. "It doesn't matter now anyway. You will be shot as spies and save me the bother of feeding you."

"When do you expect we will be shot Lieutenant?" Alan asked.

"I'd say in about one week from now, at dawn. We're going to be moving the prisoners to another location soon and you won't be going."

"Yes, you said that already," Danny said.

"What's that smart guy? Do you take me for a fool?"

"Yes sir. I mean no sir. I don't want to be shot by any fool of course, sir," Danny said.

With that comment, the Lieutenant turned and fled, before anyone could see that his face had turned scarlet in anger.

"Now what do we do? It looks like Elizabeth got her wish after all. We've safe and sound, until we get shot. Maybe the rescue will be a day late. Do we really know anything? Alan, what if history has already changed? Maybe the British found our bodies here and shipped them back to Upper Canada for a heroes' burial. That would explain why our graves ended up in Newark. That's what Elizabeth said, wasn't it?" Danny said.

"Take it easy Danny. If you feel this was a trap all along; then Elizabeth could be an American ghost," Alan said, as he reconsidered Danny's loyalty towards Elizabeth.

"Really Alan, you've been reading too many mysteries lately. I don't think Elizabeth would drag us all the way back to the past to play tricks on us," Danny said.

"Even if I did trick you, I would be stuck in the past with you," Elizabeth said, appearing out of nowhere. "If you don't take that American chess set back to the future, we'll all have to haunt this fort together for evermore.

Don't forget it was the angel without a name that asked you to come here. He's keeping an eye on all of us and maybe he will help us get to heaven. However, he is not going to allow us to go back home without that chess set. It's too important."

"Elizabeth! I guess that answers your question Danny. Hey, where is she anyway? I can't see her?" Alan said.

"Over here silly. I'm right behind you," Elizabeth said. Elizabeth materialized in her best Sunday dress.

"Are you going to church? You look very pretty," Danny said.

"No, I'm just happy that you made it to prison without getting shot. That was a close call."

"Maybe you can borrow the General's chess set while we sit here in this cold and damp cell waiting for the firing squad. I'd like to make myself at home you know," Alan said.

"Yes, of course. Why didn't you say so," Elizabeth said. The boys could barely contain themselves as a beautiful oak table and two chairs appeared along with the American General's chess set. "Of course we'll have to keep returning it to him. We don't want the General to get upset with us, do we?"

"Elizabeth, this is crazy. Why don't you just help us to escape and we'll run across the river and hide out until after the British capture the fort. That would be better than facing a firing squad," Alan said.

"The chess set is too evil. It contains many bad spirits. We must take it with us at the last moment. If we try to take it now, we may never return."

"Why didn't we take it in the first place Elizabeth?" Danny said.

"Because the spirits from Colonel Butler's chess set have only begun training and preparing for the invasion, since you brought the first set back to the future. Before that, they were in checkmate. Remember? Once we grab the American chess set, the spirits of Butler's Rangers will be able to remove the negativity from it and wipe out the evil spirits. However, as long as the American chess set remains in the past, in the fourth dimension, the evil spirits will be able to gain power from it and go to the future and checkmate the British position again, the same way a ghost walks into your home, through a portal. Butler's Barracks will also continue to be a trap for the unwary. The victims will continue to disappear into the fourth dimension and be transported to the past, where they will likely been apprehended as spies and shot. The torment of Newark will replay itself, again and again, for all of eternity."

"It sounds like that American General has created a living hell in the fourth dimension," Alan said.

"The evil spirits took advantage of a good situation. They also knew that we were coming," Elizabeth said, as she shrugged her shoulders.

"They seem to be rushing our funerals as well," Alan said.

"Not really. They're enjoying their little game. But I think we've got company; so I'm off for a bit. I'll return the General's belongings, so you won't have to explain how they ended up in your cell," Elizabeth said.

An American soldier from the corridor was blaring that the General was looking for his chess set. The American soldier stopped right outside of their cell. There was the jingle jangle of keys; then the door opened.

"I thought I heard voices coming from this cell. It sounded like a young girl's voice. I must be hearing things," the old soldier said, as he looked into their cell. The old fellow had a pallid face with deep lines and he had the looks of a haunted man. "The General is in a foul mood. His chess set has vanished again. If you ask me, he should get another set. I don't want to hear another peep from the two of you tonight either. This place is giving me the creeps."

"Is the General missing anything else soldier?" Alan asked.

"It's a funny thing, now that you've asked. He's missing his fine table set as well. It's a beautiful oak set with a table and a couple of chairs. He's very proud of that set. I can't quite figure out how furniture can disappear around here. If you ask me, there are spirits here. My grandfather's tales as a soldier in Fort Niagara during the War of Independence also convinced me that the phantoms have been haunting this fort since the French occupation. With the fort being occupied by British, French and American soldiers during past conflicts, I sometimes think that they still fight each other on the other side," the old soldier said.

"Tell us about the fort then, soldier," Danny said, hoping to pass the time with some interesting conversation.

"You boys don't look like British spies to me, but you stay over on your side of this cell and I'll stay on mine and I'll tell you a story about the ghosts at this fort," the soldier said, as he started to relax. "It happened on October 31st on the night of the full night, last fall." The soldier sighed and took a deep breath. "I'm the only one who heard them; but I can tell you, I still have nightmares. The other soldiers at this fort won't talk about it either. But they know the truth of the matter," the old soldier insisted.

As if to find courage, he reached into his inside pocket of his frock and pulled out a slim metal container. He popped the corked top and took a long swig. He began to compose himself and breath easier. Then he went still. He just stared ahead like he was dead. There was no movement at all. Dandy felt betrayed. Not only had they missed a good story; they would probably have to escape again before they were executed on the spot for murdering an American soldier. Danny began to wonder, if he could help the old gentleman. Perhaps, he could save his life. Danny got up and began to move towards the soldier.

"Now you boys don't try anything foolish. I've been a soldier all of my life and I'd hate to have to tell the General about the accident that you boys had down here in this dark cell," the old soldier said, as he sat forward with his musket and bayonet trained on them.

"Don't worry sir. We'd like to hear your story," Danny said, as moved backwards and tripped over himself. Then he flopped down hard in the corner. He stared at the old soldier; then he looked at Alan in disbelief.

"As I said, it was the end of October. On that night, there was a special celebration at the fort. Much of the harvest had been completed earlier than expected. Everyone was in a good mood with the celebration and all. There was plenty of beer, wine, gin and whiskey to be had. It was before we had so many prisoners down here. The General has been rounding up more and more spies these days. Anyhow, you might say I had too much of the spirits as well. I was looking for a nice quiet place to rest, so I came down here to this very cell where you boys are right now."

"That's interesting sir. Please go on," Alan said, encouraging the old timer to continue.

"Well, I thought I'd been sleeping half the night, but it was really only a few minutes because it happened around midnight."

"What happened, sir?" Danny asked.

"The ghosts came. That's what happened." He sat right back against the wall and tipped his head right back. The whiskey washed down his throat like a drainpipe. "That's better. Yes sir, they were real spirits alright. There were two of them. One was a beautiful young woman and the other was a girl. The girl spoke to me and told me that it was a mistake to attack the British and that she and her sister would take away the soldiers' uniforms, so that they would not be able to fight the British anymore." He howled with laughter and snickered like a madman. "It's okay. I'm as sober as a judge. Don't you see? That's what happened."

"What happened then sir," Danny said.

“It happened just like the ghost said it would. That’s what happened. In the morning at reveille, there wasn’t one stitch of uniform in the fort. The uniforms had completely vanished, every one of them gone. The General himself was at the fort that morning doing an inspection. He had just walked into the fort to find that not one soldier was in uniform. Most of the soldiers were running around in their underwear. All of them had left their civilian clothes behind. Even the extra uniforms were missing.” The old soldier paused and chuckled; then he slumped back into his corner, with a vacant expression on his pale face. He spoke in a slow and determined manner. “The ghosts also warned me that if we caused any more trouble at Newark, then they would return. I have a strong feeling, if we don’t leave this fort soon; then we’re all going to be dead.”

“It’s too bad the General won’t listen to you soldier,” Alan said.

“I don’t think the General would listen to anyone who believes in ghosts,” the old soldier said, as he got up and straightened himself out. Then he unlocked the cell door and let himself out. He paused on the other side of the door. Then, he turned around and spoke to the boys again, through the bars of the cell window. “I don’t wish anything to happen to you boys; but war is war.”

“Don’t worry about us chum. Watch out for yourself. Leave this place as soon as possible. It will soon be a place of death,” Alan said.

“Those are strange words for a young lad,” the old soldier said, as he shrugged his shoulders and left.

They could hear him shuffle down the narrow passage. Eventually, his mutterings grew faint. They were alone again in the semi-darkness. However, there was always enough light from the lantern located in the passage, to play a game of chess.

“I’ve got an idea,” Alan said, after the old soldier was far enough away.

“Anything is better than sitting here and rotting,” Danny said.

"We'll need Elizabeth's help. I think we can start by getting that chess set in our hands again, until we are released."

"You mean, if we are released," Danny corrected him.

"You really are an optimist, aren't you Danny."

"Have you boys been enjoying yourselves," a voice from nowhere said.

"Elizabeth. Where are you?" Danny said.

"Right here beside you," Elizabeth said, as she slowly materialized in a silky white full dress.

"Hey, you really do look like a ghost Elizabeth. What's going on?" Alan demanded.

"That's the whole point. It's time to haunt Fort Niagara. The General is staying at the fort tonight. We won't get another opportunity like this again. This is really going to be fun, don't you think?"

"Think? All I can think about is the firing squad. They're going to line us up and shoot us down in cold blood in a few days time and all you can think about is having a good time," Alan said.

"Really Alan, I understand you have concerns, but we need to take one step at a time, don't we? First comes the haunting of the General and that involves you."

"What involves us? We're not ghosts like you. Sometimes I wonder about my sanity Elizabeth," Alan said.

"No, you're not a ghost, at least not yet. But you can use telepathy and project yourself as being one. You should be ready to perform in the grand finale, in about four days from now. Three ghosts are better than one, don't you agree? I've got to go now and pay the General a visit," Elizabeth said, as she tried to cover up her mischievous smile with her hand. "The General is not going to like it one bit."

The American General had decided to stay at Fort Niagara the following evening; the day after Newark was burnt to the ground. He returned to his comfortable office like he usually did for a long look at his maps; then he changed his mind and decided to go for a quick snack of cheese and wine.

As he walked from his quarters, towards the officers' kitchen, he heard the wild whoop of a bird, somewhere beyond the fort. He considered the vast woods surrounding both Fort George and Fort Niagara. Where there are woods, there are Indians. He shuddered with the idea that the Indians might try and surround his fort. A snack would not be enough to cheer him up now. He needed to return to the security of his office and take some stronger medicine.

He arrived back at his office and was stunned to find his oak table, two chairs and a chess set missing. Moreover, this was the second time that his chess set had gone missing, since Newark was destroyed.

The General was livid. He called out the guard to search the fort for the missing furniture. Now he had a real swine to deal with besides the British. Where could the swine hide his furniture, he thought to himself? There is no way anyone could hide something that large in Fort Niagara.

He sat heavily in his favourite posh chair; but soon became restless. So he got out his map of Newark, took it over to the fireplace and threw it onto the flames. The map curled up like it was alive and it flew from the flames like a wounded animal. The stag's head which hung over the fireplace looked down at the burning map of Newark as it wriggled in agony. Finally, the burnt map crumbled into grey ashes. At that moment, the large black eyes of the stag ceased to reflect the sorrow and pain of the burning town. They now stared at the General in disdain.

The General was dismayed that the burning map should jump from his fireplace and leave a large ashen mark on his nice blue rug. In a fit of temper, he topped up his wine and drank it down in one gulp. Then he drank another glass full of the red ruby wine and another. Soon, he had a silly grin on his face, with the absurd thought of how the President of the United States would reward him for his victory at Newark, until he realized that he wasn't alone.

"General George Taylor of the New York Militia," the unseen voice said.

"Who said that?" the General replied, as he stood up sharply. "Don't you know who I am General?" the voice spoke again.

"I beseech you to show yourself. Come out now, or I'm have you arrested and shot," the General said, as he began to lose his composure.

"Oh you will, will you. I think not General George Taylor. You've done enough shooting and burning, haven't you now? I think that you'd better listen to me instead," the voice continued.

"Yes, yes, what do you want?" the General asked, as he became exasperated from talking with the space around his office.

"Nothing sir, I only came by to see if you needed anything," the Sergeant said.

The General was startled by the sudden appearance of his most trusted senior non-commissioned officer.

"Nothing Sergeant, sorry, I was thinking about my furniture and the chess set," the General replied.

"Yes, a fine set of chess and oak it is sir. If you will permit me sir, I see you're in the middle of a game already. If that will be all sir, goodnight," the Sergeant said, as he saluted, turned sharply and marched out.

The General felt like he was losing his grip as he looked down at the chess set, his two favourite game chairs and the oak table. They were all in place, except for one disturbing thing. The British chess pieces had the American general (king) in checkmate.

General George Taylor steadied himself with a strong shot of gin which he kept in a hidden desk drawer. He felt faint and weak at first; but within a minute of consuming a few ounces of the strong gin, he was able to shape up. Perhaps his furniture and chess set had been there all along and he was hearing things.

The General's pocket watch indicated the time as midnight. The pale moon shone fully into his office. He had never noticed the moon before. Tonight, it seemed to enlarge every shadow, as he began to blow out the lanterns and the candles.

As he got set to blow out the last of the lanterns, he hesitated for an instance. In the back of his office, he could detect a soft, orb-like white glow. It moved from the moonlight into a corner of the room, until something larger appeared.

"General George Taylor. You weren't thinking of going to bed yet, were you? I think we have a few things to talk over," the shadow said.

The General shuddered and fell backwards into his posh chair.

He was barely able to move from his shaking.

"Please leave me alone. This is only a bad dream and I want to go to sleep," the General said to the shadow in the corner.

"You will go to sleep my friend. You will go to sleep. But first, you must do as I ask," the shadow replied.

"Yes anything. Just let me sleep," the General pleaded.

"Very well, you will remove your two favourite chairs, the oak table and the chess set from your office and you will give them to the two young British prisoners that you captured last night. Is that clear?" the shadow demanded.

"Yes, very clear, thank you. It will be done tomorrow. Good night to you.

The General slept in until almost noon. His soldiers didn't dare wake him. All the uniforms had disappeared again. Captain Black had sent out for more uniforms. When the General awoke around noon, he found a note on his desk with the message to remember his promise. It was signed "THE SHADOW." He laughed and threw it in the garbage.

That was to be his last laugh. He should have listened to "the shadow."

General George Taylor was very angry when he heard that his men had to run around in their underwear and old clothes. There was even a report that a soldier had dressed up as a woman. The General would be the laughing stock of Buffalo by the time he returned there in the spring. He was determined to get to the bottom of whoever was causing problems at the fort.

It was late at night again and the General had one too many drinks of whiskey, gin and wine for the second night in a row. He had just finished playing chess against himself and had the satisfaction of cornering the red-coated general. He turned around for a split second, to sip his whiskey, when he noticed that the red- coated general was no longer in checkmate. He looked carefully at the game again. He could have sworn that he checked the red-coated general. He tried to re-position his pieces, until it finally dawned on him that the blue-coated general was in checkmate.

"What the devil is going on here?" he said out loud. "I could have sworn the game was the other way around."

"What the devil indeed General," the unseen voice said. "You shouldn't be surprised."

"Please leave me alone. I'll do anything," the General wailed.

"That's what you said last night," the voice replied. "Now you will have to listen to me. You didn't do what I told you to do and look what has happened to your men. I'm going to leave you with three warnings. The first warning is that you must move your chess set from here to the prisoner's cell as I told you, before you retire. The second is that bayonets are trump. The third is that you may expect advice from those who know you well. Farewell General George Taylor."

"But I don't understand. Wait."

But it was too late. Elizabeth's spirit had left the General to his own devices. The General wanted to get the chess set out of his sight, so he asked the Sergeant to remove the furniture and the chess set to the prisoners' cell. The Sergeant was beginning to wonder about the General's sanity, after he complained about the chess set being missing previously.

"Sergeant, before you go, I have a riddle to solve. What do you think bayonets are trump means?" the General said.

"It sounds like a game to me," the Sergeant replied. "I'm sorry I can't help you General. I'm not much for games."

"Neither am I, Sergeant. Neither am I. Well, what are you waiting for Sergeant? Take the accursed chess set, along with the table and the chairs. Give them to the spies we captured the other night," the General bellowed, as the Sergeant saluted.

The Sergeant removed the offending articles from the General's quarters and decided to take them down to the supervising officer's quarters for a quick game of chess with another non-commissioned officer. However, every time the American chess pieces checked the red-coated general, the reverse would occur.

Alan and Danny were both sound asleep when the Sergeant burst into their cell with the chess set and the furniture.

"Compliments of the General; but don't blame me, if it's a one- sided game," the Sergeant said, as he left in a hurry.

“What was he going on about Alan? Whoever heard of a one- sided game of chess. Elizabeth must have had something to do with this. Imagine the General handing us over the chess set without a whimper,” Danny said.

“Oh, he whimpered alright,” the unseen voice said.

“Elizabeth, how did you do it?” Alan said.

“Never mind how I did it. You fellows are going to be having some fun in a few days time. Do you remember what I said about using telepathy?”

“Yes, isn’t that something to do with sending messages to a distant place using your mind,” Danny said.

“Yes, it means that you can send images from your mind to another mind. It’s that simple,” Elizabeth said. “Well, that’s exactly what’s going to happen on the night of the attack. Good night lads.”

On the night of the impending attack on Fort Niagara, General George Taylor was sitting in his easy chair staring into mid-air, after drinking several stiff drinks of whiskey. One of his spies had said that the fort would be attacked; but there had been no reprisal for burning Newark. The General wasn’t worried about the British anymore and neither were his troops. Instead of guarding the fort, most of them were playing cards.

The General found it difficult to concentrate without his chess set. His plan was to get rid of the spies that he caught during the week and get his chess game back. Little did he realize that the British were marching across the Niagara River around midnight. Their plan was to surprise the Americans on this bitterly cold night.

He was just about ready to summon the Sergeant, when he noticed the late hour. His room seemed very chilly and he reached for a few more logs to place on the fireplace. When he looked up he saw two soldiers looking at him.

One was wearing a British general's uniform. The other was wearing a green officer's uniform.

"Who in blue blazes are you?" the American General spoke.

"Good evening General Taylor," the British General replied. "Perhaps you know who I am?"

"Yes, I believe I've seen you somewhere. But wait, you're not the British commander in this area. How did you get inside the fort?"

"Easy General, it is of no concern. You do know me. Think harder."

"No, it can't be. You have a striking resemblance to Major General Brock."

"It is the same. I am Brock's spirit and I have come on a mission of great importance."

"Speak, spirit of General Brock. Pray that you don't haunt me. I am only performing my duty, as my country demands."

"Then listen and listen well General Taylor. Does your country demand that you commit a great crime against humanity? Your feeble life isn't worth much; but I owe it to you, as one general to another that you should flee this accused place or you must share the same fate as the oppressed."

"Thank you, spirit of Brock for your guidance."

"There's one more thing General."

"Anything you wish, spirit of Brock."

"You must free the two British prisoners within the hour. The prisoners will take the chess set with them. You will also lead them to a place where they can cross the ice."

"This I will do, great spirit of Brock."

"General, there is still one more thing," said the green-coated spirit. "Bayonets are trump."

"But I don't understand good spirit," the American General said.

"You will General, you will," the green-coated spirit said. "Before you go General, there is one more spirit that you need to speak with."

"Spirits, please do I have to speak with so many spirits?"

Before the General could protest any further, the two soldier spirits were gone. A stern looking spirit took their place and walked over to the General's fireplace and stood there, with his arms folded in front of him. His uniform was British looking; yet it was of a different time. General George Taylor recognized him as the first President of America.

"General Washington, is it really you sir?" General Taylor said.

"Yes, it is you bumbling fool. Listen carefully Taylor. Chopping down cherry trees is one thing, but burning down towns is another. You will regret this action. The British will try and burn the President's home and the American people will remember your part in it General Taylor. They'll also remember the bill you ran up for those lost uniforms. If I was you, General, I would high tail it out of here fast. This fort is no place for a scoundrel. Do I make myself clear?"

"Yes, thank you sir, thank you very much. Is there anything else sir?"

"Yes Taylor there is."

"What's that, sir?"

"Bayonets are trump."

With that comment President George Washington disappeared into the fourth dimension, along the time continuum.

General Taylor ran down to the prisoner cell block, dismissed his guards and unlocked Danny and Alan's cell in person.

"What gives General? You're not going to shoot us yourself are you?" Alan asked.

"The spirits have spoken. We have to leave right away. The British will be attacking soon."

"General Taylor, I thought it was your job to protect the fort from the British," Danny said.

"That was before I talked with the spirit world," the General answered back.

"Oh, I see what you mean General. Don't worry. We'll help you to escape, if you help us. All we want is your chess set," Alan said.

"Yes, I know about the chess set and you can have it. Use it in good health. It's like loaded dice, if you ask me," the General said. "Come on then, the British are going to attack the fort tonight and there's something about bayonets are trump."

As the General and the boys were leaving the fort by the back way, they could hear the soft whispers of the British soldiers.

"General, you'd better stick close to us. It might not be too healthy to wander in the woods," Alan said.

At the sound of woods, the General became terrified.

"Do you think the woods are full of Indians?" the General asked.

"It wouldn't surprise me General. There are a lot of woods around here. You had better stick close to us," Alan said.

Near the front gate they could hear some American soldiers playing a game of cards. One of the soldiers asked what was trump. In response, a British soldier said, "bayonets are trump," just before the Americans were rushed.

The British used bayonets throughout the fort in order to utilize the element of surprise. Not one soldier fired a musket during the raid on Fort Niagara.

The General and the boys cleared the fort without running into any of the invading forces. They walked along the frozen river far enough, in order to cross on the thicker ice.

"It's okay to cross here lads," the American General said.

"You wouldn't just be saying that, would you General?" Danny asked.

"If you walk across at this point, you will walk right up to Fort George. You can't go wrong."

"General, before you go, there's someone I want you to meet. Elizabeth, are you there?"

"General Taylor can you hear me?" the unseen voice said.

"It's that voice again; the one that told me about the bayonets and the chess set," the General exclaimed, in bewilderment.

"General, I just want to say that you did your duty and that you should never return to either Fort George or Fort Niagara again. The spirits of the forts would never allow the likes of you to intrude upon them again," the voice said.

"Yes, great spirit, is there anything else?"

"Yes, you must provide as much help as you can to the American people. They will need your help because of what you've done. They will be attacked like you attacked the British. There is nothing that can be done to prevent it. Do not commit evil deeds again. Do you hear me General Taylor?" the voice said.

"Yes, please forgive me. I beseech you."

"Yes, you are forgiven. Now go, and never come back here. Go now," the voice commanded.

The General ran within an inch of his life. He never turned his back until daybreak.

"Cross the river quickly and proceed to Butler's cabin," Elizabeth said. "It will be dawn soon. You must be at the appointed spot or you will be stuck in 1813 forever."

The two lads crossed the frozen river and walked up the steep hill, in the deep snow, towards Fort George. They weren't expecting anyone to be on duty, but they were wrong.

"Hold and be identified," the British soldier said.

"British," Alan said. "We're reporting to Butler's Barracks."

"Butler's Barracks—there is no such place. Old Colonel Butler used a little cabin nearby for his meetings. His old barracks was destroyed before the war."

"That's my mistake Sergeant. Butler's cabin is where we want to go. They're going to rebuild Butler's Barracks after the war is over," Alan said, as the confused Sergeant rubbed his chin a few times in the cold, crisp morning air.

"What's your rank anyhow? I've never seen you around these parts before. Let me see your uniform. It's certainly a fancy one," the Sergeant said, as he looked at Alan's uniform under his winter frock.

"I've seen that uniform before. I don't know how you got it lad; but the General was buried in it. It's also got a hole over the heart where he was shot. I was there when General Brock got sniped. I don't understand what it is you want lad. It seems beyond me."

"I know how you feel Sergeant. It's a bit beyond me too; since I wasn't wearing it before I met you. But if you escort us to the cabin, I will try to explain part of it. Let me tell you one thing. All of this is to secure the future of this country, as the protectors wanted it. General Brock, Colonel Butler, General Wolfe, Captain James FritzGibbon, Chief Tecumseh and Laura Second would stand by me this very minute, if they could and help me to do this one final deed," Alan said.

"As you say lad, it is well beyond me," the Sergeant said, as they approached Butler's cabin by Fort George.

"Don't be alarmed Sergeant, but my brother here and I will be returning to a different time. Fort George will fall into ruins when the British Army leaves Upper Canada; however, all the forts of this time will be rebuilt or repaired. They will continue to exist for all eternity to remind us of our history and our heritage. But now, it is almost daylight."

"It is time Alan and Danny. Farewell Sergeant," the unseen voice said.

The Sergeant gazed in amazement, at the exact image of General Brock and an officer called FitzGibbon. He thought that FitzGibbon was still alive; so how could he be in two places at the same time? Was this Alan really the spirit of General Brock? He began to wonder. Then he heard the voice of a little girl which he recognized at once. She was reported missing when the Americans invaded Newark, several months before.

"Remember this day Sergeant. You have indeed seen the spirits of those from the future, who were once the soldiers of your time. Farewell again," the voice said.

The lads and Elizabeth found themselves back in the present just before the dawn.

"There's one last thing that you need to do," Elizabeth said.

"I knew there was going to be another catch. I knew it," Danny said.

"Take it easy Danny. Elizabeth hasn't let us down yet," Alan said. "Hey Elizabeth, I'm still in my general's uniform and Danny is still Captain FitzGibbon; or is it Lieutenant FitzGibbon? Maybe you haven't been promoted yet Danny."

"That's very funny Alan. You always talked like a big shot general. What's rank got to do with it? Back in our time, you're just Alan Hood the re-enactor," Danny said.

"Yes, but I can re-enact anyone I choose, can't I?" Alan replied.

"If you two would settle down for one minute, we can finish this. I took the American chess set from you and stored it at Fort George in the fourth dimension, where no one will find it. But we have to perform one more ceremony to stop the evil spirits from returning," Elizabeth said.

"Okay Elizabeth, let's get on with it," Danny said.

"I've even got one with me," Elizabeth said.

"That's a drum Elizabeth. What gives?" Alan said.

"For your information, it's a Grenadier drum and you must start beating it with these two sticks as hard as you can. Good luck."

Elizabeth disappeared; but the lads were left standing in full uniform with their Grenadier drum.

"Go ahead Danny. It's your turn to attract attention. We'll probably be back in jail before too long; but at least this time, we won't be shot as spies," Alan said.

"I hope Elizabeth is still watching over us" Danny replied. "Most of all, I hope she's not playing any ghostly tricks. By the time I hit this drum a few times, I will be signaling, every police patrol in Niagara-on-the-Lake to come and take us away. Here it goes."

Danny hit the drum for about ten minutes, until he saw the red flashing lights appear about three hundred yards away. The sun was just appearing over the horizon, as the police arrived.

"Did you boys see a nut with a large drum in a uniform parading around here? We received a phone call about ten minutes ago that there were two soldiers beating the life out of a huge old drum. I can't figure it out. They must have been drinking. Well, thanks anyway. I expect you two are working at the fort. I recognize you. Let me know if you see anything suspicious. Take care."

The police officer left.

"What happened to the uniforms and the drum?" Alan said.

"It was the angel without a name. He took the uniforms and the drum back into the spirit world. He also said that we should head towards Fort George this morning and have dinner with our parents at the Colonel's restaurant tonight," Danny said.

"It suits me. How can you argue with an angel without a name," Alan agreed.

"Maybe that's why he chose that name," Danny said, as both boys laughed on it.

Play Phantom For Me

This little ghostly adventure took place during the quiet, early morning hours, just after daybreak. Alan and Danny Hood showed up at Butler's Barracks in uniform and were told to play a Grenadier drum, in order to prevent evil spirits from returning to Fort George. Unfortunately, the military signal drum was also heard by a disgruntled local, who called the police. But the quick thinking angel without a name, hide the uniforms and the drum, before the boys could be blamed for disturbing the peace.

With a sigh of relief, the boys walked the back paths towards Fort George; thus avoiding the town and any more trouble. Perhaps they could find a nice spot near the fort and have a rest. The shops wouldn't be open for a few hours and they had no lodgings or anywhere to go in particular. As they walked onwards towards Fort George, they discussed their future plans and how much they were looking forward to seeing their parents later on, at the Colonel's restaurant.

"Hey Danny, that was a close call. It would not have been a good show, if Mom and Dad had to bail us out of jail on our last day in Niagara-on-the-Lake." Danny didn't appear to be listening, as they approached Fort George. "What's up Danny? You look a little preoccupied."

"Didn't you notice Alan?

"Notice what, little brother? Do you think I'm a mind reader?"

"Look over there Alan. The front gates of the fort are open. There're never open at this time of day," Danny explained. "I can see a soldier there as well. Let's have a look and see what's going on."

Alan knew everyone at the fort, but he didn't recognize the guard. The guard came alert, as the boys approached the gate.

"Welcome to Fort George gentlemen," the guard said. "They're waiting for you at the officers' quarters."

Alan thanked the soldier, who saluted both him and Danny as they walked onto the vacant parade grounds inside the fort.

"That soldier isn't wearing a regulation uniform," Danny whispered to Alan. "He looks like he's dressed for the American Revolution."

"Yes, I agree with you on that one Danny. Maybe we should ask him what it's all about."

As the boys turned back to look for the soldier, they could see no sign of him. He wasn't in the sentry-box and there was no possible way he could have walked away; since there were no buildings close to the gate or the sentry-box. The front gate was shut as well. The boys walked over to examine it and noticed that it was bolted from the inside. The boys understood that the soldier didn't just shut the gate and leave the fort.

"Now what do we do?" Danny said.

"We do what we should do," Alan replied. "Let's see what's cooking at the officers' kitchen, now that we're in the fort."

There was some interesting music coming from the officers' quarters. The boys could hear "Rule Britannia" with lots of high- spirited singing, as they opened the front door.

"Hey, what's going on?" Danny shouted. "I heard music in here a few seconds ago."

"I did too Danny," Alan replied. "Maybe we should beat it out of here, before we get hijacked and transported back to the past again."

"Alan, don't look now but there's something in the mirror. It's that old-fashioned ghost lady that they all talk about on the ghost tour and she looks like someone we know who works at the fort," Danny said, as he stared at the mirror. "She wants us to come closer. Alan, I know she's a ghost and not a real person; otherwise why would she be stuck in the mirror? Alan let's get out of here."

But Alan couldn't move away from the image in the mirror. He stood there and stared at the smiling lady. The ghost lady beckoned Alan to come closer, one final time. Now Alan was right in front of the mirror.

"Snap out of it Alan. It's a trick. She's a ghost lady. Run for it," Danny pleaded.

But Alan paid no attention to Danny's concerns. Instead, he took half a dozen steps backwards and came to attention. Then the most remarkable thing happened. The lady disappeared and the image of a soldier in a green uniform appeared in the mirror instead. He was a very distinguished looking chap too. He looked up and down at Alan like he was inspecting him and he even threw a glance in Danny's direction which rooted him to the spot.

"Rest easy boys; this is Colonel Butler speaking. As long as the Rangers have gentlemen like you boys around, we'll rest easy. But if anything should change our minds; the officers' quarters may not be the best place for visitors, if you know what I mean."

Alan seemed to snap out of it first. He came to attention and saluted the Colonel.

"Yes sir, everything will be okay with the fort Colonel. We'll look after things for you; won't we Danny?"

"Yes sir, Alan and I will honour the Rangers as long as Fort George exists. You can depend on it Colonel," Danny agreed.

"Thank you boys, I knew I could depend on you. I'll be seeing you soon."

The Colonel's image disappeared in the mirror and the boys looked at each other.

"I don't know about you Danny; but that was a close call."

"What do you mean Alan?"

"Don't tell me that you forgot about the mission that the Colonel sent us on recently?"

"Now that you mention it, I am getting a little homesick," Danny said, as he stared out the window. "Look Alan, the front gates are open again.

"It looks like the Colonel is on the level with us. Mission accomplished," Alan said. "The Colonel's a great guy; but when we go to that restaurant with Mom and Dad later on, I hope he doesn't stare or wink at us. I find that portrait of him as spooky as the ghost himself."

"You've got a point Alan. I think the Colonel is going to give us time off for good behavior now that we've accomplished everything he wanted us to do. Maybe he can rest easy for a change."

"Somehow I don't think the Colonel will ever rest easy, as long as there are visitors to the fort."

"Who said that the visitors want to see him?" Danny asked.

"Let's just say that if you want to feel lucky in this fort, it might be an idea to have the Colonel on your side."

"The Colonel sure knows how to make your day," Danny agreed, as both boys laughed and headed out of the deserted fort.

***

Richard Hood had an amazing story to tell his boys at the restaurant later that day. He had bought a War of 1812 chess set for Alan's birthday and had put it in his filing cabinet, so it would be a surprise. Just before he was leaving home with Sarah, he found the entire chess set on his desk with the British Army defending an advancing American Army. He swore that he heard that the chess pieces say that they did not want to be locked up.

Alan and Danny looked at each other. Maybe something had gone wrong with their mission.

"The same thing happened to me a long time ago. It was another War of 1812 chess set. Everything was fine once the set was displayed in a place of prominence," Richard Hood said, being somewhat amused. The boys sighed with relief. "Why don't you boys say hello to old Colonel Butler before we go home. His portrait is reputed to be haunted."

"If you say so Dad, come on Danny, let's say hello to the Colonel," Alan said, with a twinkle in his eye.

Both of the boys marched over towards the Colonel's portrait. Alan caught Danny's attention and winked at him. Then he turned back to the portrait. To his dismay, the Colonel was smiling at him. Alan almost ran for his life.

"Don't worry Alan. It's the angel again," Danny said. "He's played a little joke on you. He wanted you to know that everything is okay with Elizabeth, the Colonel and the rest of Butler's spirits. Best of all, no one should be transported back to the past for the time being."

High Plains Phantoms

It was a Halloween ghost tour that the boys would never forget. Alan and Danny Hood had missed their summer of adventure, so much that they came back for the special ghost tour in October. They also missed Elizabeth, the spirit who had helped them with their summer mission. With Elizabeth's help, the boys were able to escape from Fort Niagara during the War of 1812, before they were to be shot as British spies. The boys were able to re-cross the border and make it back into their own time, with the captured American chess set which was needed at Fort George.

Back in their own time, the boys decided to pay tribute to old Colonel Butler, at the restaurant where his spirit was said to be resting. Alan made the mistake of commenting on how run-down Butler's Barracks had become, right in front of the portrait of the old Colonel. He continued with how Butler's Rangers deserved more respect and how they missed some great opportunities for battle honours during the War of 1812.

"Did you see that?" Danny exclaimed. "See what? Alan answered.

"I swear that the old Colonel's eyes rolled back. Maybe the paint is beginning to peel on his portrait, with the dust gathering from the new subdivisions that are being built here," Danny said, as he looked out the window at the cleared fields and the piles of dirt across the street. "I really think the restaurant owners should take more care with their prize possession here. They sure don't know how to look after anything older than thirty years in this country. They sure have no spirit."

"The only spirits I want to see are those that belong at the fort. After all, that is what the ghost tour is all about," Alan said.

“Well Colonel, we’ll see you at the fort later, if that’s what you want. Bye for now,” Danny said, as he saluted the Colonel and did an about turn.

Alan and Danny both marched out of the restaurant together like they were still students practicing drill and serving in the British Army at Fort George during the summer months. The portrait smiled as the two boys exited from the building.

The two boys joined the last ghost tour which was to finish at midnight. They were disappointed that Elizabeth did not show up. In fact, there had been no signs of ghosts at all.

It was almost midnight as the tour passed the guardhouse. The guardhouse was not a normal stop for discussion; but there had been an incident earlier that evening; so, Danny and Alan’s tour guide decided to share that information with his group.

“Earlier this evening a tour guide noticed a strange green light within the guardhouse here. When he looked more closely with his lantern, he thought he could see the face of a man in uniform staring out. His first reaction was to tell his group, but then he thought he might panic with them; so he went quickly to the door to see if it was unlocked. He found the door to be secured. Then he gathered his strength to look inside the guardhouse. After unlocking the door, he went into the small building and looked everywhere for a sign of intruders. The building was seen to be unoccupied. He locked up and took his group away. After moving twenty feet from the guardhouse, he felt a strange sensation that someone or something was looking at him from behind. His skin began to prickle and he felt most uncomfortable. He turned quickly and asked his group if they could see anything in the guardhouse. No one could, except he could see three soldiers looking back at him through the window. Before he could say, “Are you sure?” they disappeared. He took his group outside of the fort and went straight to the ghost tour leader, who tried to calm him down. Instead of going home right after the tour, the leader suggested to the unnerved tour guide that he join his group, so he could calm himself before leaving the fort. There's one more thing. I'm that tour guide. I decided that I would not only have to stay the evening; I would have to work the late shift, if I was ever to have the nerve to work here again. If anyone is brave enough to go into that guardhouse at midnight and prove to me that it is not haunted, I will take back my story."

"We'll do that for you. We know our way around the guardhouse. Come on Danny, let's take a peep inside," Alan said.

"Do you need the lantern?" the tour guide suggested.

"No. I don't want to spoil any of the fun. We'll be right back out. So don't worry. If you don't mind, perhaps you could shine that lantern by the window," Alan added, as he stepped inside the deep gloom of the guardhouse.

"You should not have volunteered," the invisible voice said.

"Who said that? Was that you, Alan? It didn't sound like your voice," Danny whispered.

"It's me silly. It's Elizabeth. Who else were you expecting? You came here to see me, didn't you?"

"In a way, I mean yes of course; but we really didn't expect you to sneak-up on us like this," Alan said.

"Well, how else do you expect me to sneak-up on you, if you please? Anyhow you're in big trouble. You've changed history by involving Butler's Rangers in the Battle of Beaver Dams."

"Hey Alan, it looks dark out there. What did that tour guide do with the lantern? I can't see any light," Danny said.

"Hey, you're right. Maybe we'd better step out and find out what's going on. Hey, what's this? The door to this jail is locked. Hey Danny, we've been locked up inside. Is this some kind of a joke Elizabeth? We're getting tired of being locked up," Alan said.

"It's no joke. This hour is still midnight in your time, and you may be returned to your time, if the Rangers succeed."

"What do you mean succeed? Are we in Fort George or not? It should be easy enough to get out of here," Danny said.

"Yes, it might be easy to get shot for escaping. During the Battle of Beaver Dams, the Americans controlled Fort George. Look at your uniforms," she commanded.

"I thought this shirt was getting a bit stiff around the collar Danny. It looks like we're wearing our old uniforms," Alan remarked.

"I almost forgot to tell you that you're going to be shot at sunrise. The Americans don't know you're in jail yet; but when they discover you in the morning; you will both be wearing Ranger uniforms. They will be happy to shoot you," Elizabeth added.

"What the heck has old Butler done anyhow? What wrong with the Americans? They don't just shoot soldiers for nothing," Alan asked.

"Yes, you are correct. But the spirits of Butler's Rangers that were killed by American forces are avenging themselves. There is a breakdown in discipline in the American ranks. I don't have to tell you what that means in this environment. Obviously, the American commander will want to maintain discipline in the ranks by showing force of arms."

"Is there anything we can do Elizabeth?" Alan asked.

Elizabeth ignored the comment and continued. "At this moment Butler's Rangers are approaching the fort. The American soldiers will soon come face to face with the spirits of Butler's Rangers. I can sense them coming. Listen!" She paused, then continued with her story. "The spirits of Butler's Rangers have helped an old friend FitzGibbon and his Bully Boys to capture over five hundred American soldiers. Many of those captured American soldiers saw skeletons in green uniforms coming out of the mist. Moreover, the soldiers with bony faces were perceived to be quite hostile. The American commanders were saying, it was only the Indians playing tricks. In reality, the skull faced warriors were the spirits of Butler's Rangers. Their bodies turn to bone at night, in the mist and in fog. Also, in any smoky conditions like battles, they will revert to their skeleton forms. Listen! The American soldiers are screaming and deserting their posts. The Rangers are in the fort. They're approaching, closer and closer."

Very slowly, the outside door to the guardhouse opened. There was the click of a lock; but no key; then the door to the prison cell opened. Alan looked pale. Danny stepped back like he wanted to walk out the back of the cell. They both turned to look for Elizabeth; but Elizabeth was not there.

A light shone in the guardhouse and the tour guide came rushing in.

"I waited a couple of minutes; then I opened the outside door. I thought I hear a young girl's voice. I checked all of the cells; but there was no one there. I rushed out of the building because my nerves were acting up again. Fortunately, I left the outside door open and several witnesses saw floating green orbs go into one of the cells. That's when I knew you weren't playing a joke; so I composed myself and ran back inside and opened this cell door. Did you see anything?"

"No, but we're grateful that you decided to come in the guardhouse when you did. It must have taken some courage," Alan said. "I can't say we can answer all of your questions either; since some strange things happened in here. If you don't mind, I think we would like to leave the fort as soon as possible, unless you want to see something you really don't want to see," Alan suggested.

"Not on your life mate," the tour guide said, deciding that he had no more courage to spare.

The tour group rushed from the fort; but the tour guide couldn't resist that one final look back. He swore he saw several bony hands waving back at him from the guardhouse.

Phantom Without a Name

"What do you mean our house is haunted?" Alan's father said. "Devils, ghosts and angels, you say. This really is too much, Alan."

Alan looked down at the floor, as his father continued his lecture on supernatural.

"This is the 21st century Alan. We don't believe in such silliness now, do we? Angels too, you say. For heaven's sake Alan, don't you realize that according to what you've just told me, this house should be full of spirits by now, should it not?"

Alan was a very perceptive boy of nine years of age. He could not be so easily perturbed by his father's close mindedness. He just stuck out his chest a bit more and he brought up his head to stare at his father eye to eye. His father knew that look of betrayal, and he decided to break it off.

"Well, it's still poppycock as far as I'm concerned," Alan's father said as he sat back down at his desk.

Richard Hood had removed the whole episode from his mind as he settled down comfortably to some more pleasant task. He was just about to reach for a pen when the bamboo hall mirrors blew off of the wall, just outside of his office.

"What in heaven's name is going on around here? It sounds like we're under attack."

"It's okay Dad. It's only an angel. He just wants to get your attention. He says that he's from the Senior Council of Angels, but you can just call him the angel without a name."

"You've got a good imagination, Alan and a boy needs that today above all," Richard said. "But I really have to get my work done. Since we've moved into this new house, my paychecks never seem to amount to anything. Maybe your angel friend can help me find a better paying job."

"He says all in good time, Dad. What he really wants to tell you is that you have a problem."

"Now listen, Alan, this is too much. What kind of an angel would tell anyone that they have a problem?"

"That not quite right Dad. He means that we have intruders and very soon they will start causing trouble."

"Oh really, do you mean ghosts? We'll be the talk of the town."

"Dad, I'm afraid it's a bit more serious than just a few spirits trying to move in here," Alan replied.

"I hope you and your younger brother aren't making this up Alan?"

"Dad, I think you should listen to what the angel has to say. There's a ghost called John who would like to take over your office. He's a very bad spirit. He wants you to move out now. He's got a spirit army, and they want to move your belongings from your office."

"Alan, I've had just about enough of this nonsense," was all that Richard could say as he observed his desk files creeping along the floor in his office, towards the den.

The ghost started to unplug his computer and pull out the plugs. Then the monitor appeared on the floor, screen down as if by magic. The computer mouse was the only item that had not been removed. It swung wildly from the computer cabinet back and forth like a grandfather clock after it had been knocked off of its perch. The garbage can in the office was turned upside down. His father's books began to leave their shelves one by one. Each one came forward about two feet, hung there for a moment, then dropped into the middle of the room.

"Now do you believe me, Dad? The ghost wants you to move all of your things out of your office."

"Let's go upstairs and talk Alan. Perhaps you have something after all," Richard said, as he and Alan moved upstairs to the living room. "Now, Alan, what does this angel from the Council suggest?"

"I think it would be a good idea to follow the angel's instructions Dad."

"Yes, I know Alan. But could you keep it down a bit. I don't want your mother to get wind of this. We've got enough trouble without involving her too."

"Perhaps you should tell her Dad. After all, she is part of the family."

"Maybe later Alan, if she believes any of this. First, tell me what I must do; then I'll decide whether it's important enough to tell her."

"Okay Dad. If you want to go ahead, this is what we have to do in order to defeat the evil army."

"Alan, maybe they have the wrong address. Nothing bad has ever happened in this house."

"Dad, I think they've come here because of you. You represent something important to them. The angel said that you must buy lots of toy soldiers, some music CD's of military bands, a big Grenadier drum, a War of 1812 chess set and re-enactor outfits for all of us, including Mom."

"Hey, I thought Guardian Angels were on our side?"

"What do you mean Dad? The angel is here to help."

"You mean the angel is here to help me to empty out my wallet. If your mother knew that I was spending good money on toys and party favorites, she would hit the roof. Are you sure that's everything before I go broke?"

"In fact, there are a few more things. He says you need a few red coats from the War of 1812 and a few wooden muskets will do."

"What can we do with wooden muskets?" Richard shouted, as his patience began to wear thin.

"Quiet Dad; do you want Mom to hear you shouting about the red coats and muskets? For your information, the red coats will attract the good spirits and the music will give the good spirits more power in order to fight the evil spirits. Don't worry Dad, the angel will fill out the order and submit it for you."

"How is he going to do that?"

"Through the internet—in fact, he's online right now. He knew you wouldn't want to waste any time. Time is money, right Dad?"

"Say, how is an angel going to pay for all of this Alan?"

"With a credit card—don't worry, he'll only use yours in an emergency."

"Yes, but what credit card is he using right now?"

"He's using your bank card. He wants to make sure that the order arrives on time. Don't worry, the order has been approved by the seal of the Archangels and the Creator. You can't spend your money any better than that Dad."

"Yes Alan, but I still have to pay off my credit card and it's already over the limit."

"You'll make it back Dad. The angel guarantees it."

"If angels can create miracles, why can't they just create the soldiers?"

"That would be cheating. Besides, the angel has ordered a nice present that you won't have to pay for. It's a model of a Grenadier head dress."

"I'm sure your mother will appreciate that.

"Are you going to tell her?"

"I think I'd better wait and tell her the whole story when the orders begin to arrive."

"I hope the orders arrive soon, Dad. The evil spirits are threatening to destroy your home."

The toy soldiers soon arrived. There was not one box, but two huge boxes of toy soldiers. Richard Hood couldn't believe how many toy soldiers there were. They were mainly British Army redcoats from different campaigns; however, there were some Canadian militia, some American and some French soldiers too.

Richard Hood made good on his promise to buy the rest of the required items, after visiting Fort York. He purchased two redcoats, a large Grenadier drum, a chess set representing British and American soldiers and several military march CD's. One of the soldiers at Fort York appreciated his business so much that he gave Richard half a dozen expensive books on various military uniforms from the 18th and 19th centuries. Sarah Hood still thought that Richard had gone mad; since he rarely purchased any luxury items for her like jewelry and now he was buying military items from the fort like his life depended on it.

The chess set in particular was very beautiful. After bringing it home and placing it in a filing cabinet for safekeeping, Richard was stunned to see the entire set out of its wrappings on his desk. The American pieces in blue were attacking the defensive position of the British soldiers in red.

"The spirits of the soldiers have told me that they do not want to be locked up. If you lock them up, they will go somewhere else and not help you to fight the evil spirits. However, they are still confused from fighting each other. The War of 1812 caused a great deal of hate. Still, all of the soldiers will help us tomorrow, if you put them on display in your best glass cabinet. We must destroy the evil spirits then," Alan said.

The next day there was the sound of a disembodied voice threatening to destroy the house, if the Hoods didn't do as they were told. Richard got the large Grenadier drum with two drum sticks and the two redcoats for each of his sons who proceeded to put them on. He instructed Alan to play the Grenadier's March: the battle tune which all British troops rallied to, for courage. Little Danny was only six years old; but he was old enough to signal with his field whistle, when it was time to start the military music.

The evil spirits began to fade at the sounding of the music and the drum. For the next five years, Richard continued to collect toy soldiers from different regiments for both of his sons. All the soldiers worked to protect the house from evil spirits, and their luck began to change.

Richard began to make more money at his job. Alan's marks at school began to improve and the rashes on his arms, which were due to stress, began to disappear. Danny became the most popular boy at his school and Sarah got better gifts for her birthday.

The Angel without a name was finally called back to the Council Chambers located somewhere above the ocean. He left two gifts behind.

The first was the Grenadiers headdress for Sarah which symbolized the importance of one's military heritage. It also saved Richard from severe tongue lashing for buying too many toy soldiers.

The second item that the angel left was an inukshuk. The Inuit stone figure stood about five inches tall and was placed on the highest bookshelf in Richard's office.

"The angel wanted us to have an inukshuk in order to contact him directly, if we ever need him again," Alan said.

"Amen," Richard replied.

Afterword

Butler's Rangers was a regiment of soldiers who fought on the side of the Loyalists around the time the Americans declared independence from Great Britain. I can trace my family roots on my father's side of the family back to Private Andrew Ostrander who served with them.

www.ingramcontent.com/pod-product-compliance
Lightning Source LLC
LaVergne TN
LVHW020632100826
845148LV00012B/2155

* 9 7 9 8 9 5 0 0 7 2 3 0 7 *